# FIR

For Jon

STRIPES PUBLISHING
An imprint of the Little Tiger Group
1 The Coda Centre, 189 Munster Road,
London SW6 6AW

www.littletiger.co.uk

A paperback original
First published in Great Britain in 2017
Text copyright © Sharon Gosling, 2017
Extract from *Savage Island* © Bryony Pearce, 2017
Extract fron *Charlotte Says* © Alex Bell, 2017
Cover copyright © Stripes Publishing Ltd, 2017

ISBN: 978-1-84715-823-9

A CIP catalogue record for this book is available
from the British Library.

Printed and bound in the UK.

10 9 8 7 6 5 4 3 2 1

# FIR

SHARON GOSLING

RED
EYE

If madness had a shade, it would be white.
White as far as the eye can see.
White until it reaches right around the world
and taps you on the shoulder.

You'd never think there could be
so many colours in snow. But there are.
It just takes time to see them.
Your eyes have to adjust.
Once you've been out here for a while,
you can see them.
You can see them all.

We have been out here for a long, long while.

# Chapter One

"…not going," I said.

"Don't be like that," said Dad. "This will be good for us. You'll see."

I couldn't see. Out of everything that was absolutely not apparent to me at that moment, how us moving to the middle of nowhere would be good for anything was right at the top of the list. I said this quite loudly and several times over.

"Well, if you're going to be like that, there's nothing more to say," Dad said. "We'll talk about this when you're being more reasonable."

"What about school?" I blurted.

"You'll be homeschooled."

I was so outraged that I actually snorted. "Seriously? There's not even a school? And what –" I added suddenly, realizing something – "what about the internet? Will we be online?"

Dad didn't answer that. He'd already left the room.

I had no idea why my parents wanted to do this crazy thing. I don't think I talked to them at all for the whole two months before we left. Talking wasn't something I was big on anyway and on top of that I was too angry about the whole stupid situation. Mum tried to start up a conversation once or twice but I shut that down pretty quickly. Dad kept leaving books about North Sweden and Norrbotten all over the place, probably hoping I'd get all interested and pick one up.

I didn't. I wasn't. I was pretty sure that as soon as we got up there, they'd find out what a massive mistake they'd made and come right back to Stockholm again, only now we'd be screwed because they'd sold our house. They'd never even been to visit the place they'd bought. That's how mental all this was. They dumped everything, just like that, to buy a house they'd never seen in a place they'd never been, to take on a business they had not one single clue about.

I guess, really, if I'd been less pissed off, I might have stopped to ask myself why, but I didn't. And hey, they didn't volunteer any information, either. It was as if once I'd told them in no uncertain terms that this plan was really stupid and they were dragging me there against my will, they'd decided to let me get on with being angry – like a silly kid who has a tantrum over what bowl they eat their tomato pasta out of. But this wasn't a bowl, was it? It was my *life*.

"Who the hell moves that far north?" asked Poppy as we walked home from school the next day.

"Us, apparently."

"It's going to be terrible," said Lars. "You're going to turn into a nutter. That much snow and darkness? A grade-A nutcase, that's what you'll be."

"You'll come and visit me, right?" I asked them. "In the summer?"

"You must be joking," Lars said. "And get eaten by the locals?"

"Put over their fire like a sausage on a stick?" said Poppy.

"No, thanks," they said together.

Lars and Poppy are my best friends. I have a very small life.

Anyway, a couple of weeks into September, a truck rolled up to our yellow townhouse and these men in natty blue shirts with neatly embroidered logos and tastefully matching trousers trundled out and started loading bits of our lives into it. This seemed to mean clothes, electrical equipment and knick-knacks, mainly. Most of our furniture was going into storage, which told me that for all their bravado, my parents weren't as sure about this move as they said they were. When the removal men were done, I got into the back of our 4x4 and stared at my phone, wondering why Lars and Poppy hadn't bothered to turn up to say goodbye or even text, and finally realizing what dicks my friends actually were. I put my earphones in and cranked Tool up as high as the volume would go, drowning everything out.

Through the window, I saw Mum and Dad standing on the top step of the old house. They put their arms round each other and Mum leaned her head on Dad's shoulder. She'd been doing that a lot lately, which was pretty out of character, to be honest. I'm not saying my mum's a tough nut, but she doesn't stay at home to bake cake, if you know what I mean. She's a lawyer who specializes in suing the crap out of big business on a daily basis. 'Cuddly' isn't a word I'd use to describe her. Then they shut the door to the only house I'd ever lived in, walked down the steps and got into the car.

We followed the truck out of Stockholm and drove north.

We drove north for a very, very long time.

It became clear very quickly that my parents had decided we should take the scenic route to the end of the world. I thought they might have been sensible enough to book somewhere for us to stay halfway but apparently that was too much to hope for. We stopped a few times for food and drink, and so they could share the driving. But other than that we kept going. And going. And going. And what I noted during this unbelievably boring journey was that 1) my friends still hadn't texted and 2) the trees outside the car windows grew exponentially bigger and thicker in direct contrast to how narrow the roads got. Which, I'll be honest, wasn't particularly reassuring.

I didn't voice these observations to the two so-called adults seated in front of me. They talked to each other a little on the way. They dozed. They listened to the radio. They tried to talk to me. They failed.

It was dark when I fell asleep. When I opened

my eyes again it was light and we were still going. We must have stopped again without me waking, because Mum was driving instead of Dad. My phone battery was completely dead. I could have asked Dad or Mum to plug it in for me but that would have involved speaking to them, so I didn't. The removal truck was still ahead of us, trundling along. There were still trees lining the road, punctuated by red-walled houses that looked far more cheerful than they had any right to be.

I looked at my watch. It was 9 a.m.

And still we kept going.

Eventually the trees were so thick that the road grew dark, and I got a hint of what the winter would be like. The nights were already drawing in, even in Stockholm. Up here it would be worse. In the very middle of winter, the sun would barely rise at all. We'd just get a darkness that was slightly less dark. And let's not forget the snow. Months of snow and darkness – hey, welcome to your new home!

Then, finally, the removal truck ahead of us turned off. We went from being on a reasonable road to being on an unreasonable road. I mean, I leaned forwards to look out of the windscreen and the sides of the truck were actually brushing the branches of the trees on either side. If it had got much narrower, we could have felled our own firewood on the way and wouldn't even have had to get out of the car to do it. There were times when it felt as if the trees were squashing themselves against the car as we passed. Fir trees everywhere: fir and more fir, which is, in case you hadn't noticed, the most boring tree in the world.

We drove for another hour and then the truck turned off *again*, driving past a large painted wooden sign that read *Storaskogen*. Then, suddenly, right ahead of us, I saw our new home for the first time.

It was massive. It was a mansion. It was the kind of place where you have to make an effort to count how many windows there are on each floor. It was like I was staring at a page on the 'Visit Sweden' website or something.

I swore. Quite loudly.

"Don't use that language," said Mum, on autopilot, like what I'd said wasn't entirely reasonable under the circumstances.

"These are apartments, right?" I said. "This isn't, like – the whole thing isn't ours, right?"

Dad laughed. "I have to admit, it looks bigger than the estate agent's photos. Doesn't it, darling?"

He was talking to Mum, not me, by the way. For one thing, they'd never shown *me* any photos. For another, in case you hadn't already worked it out, me and the word 'darling' aren't what you'd call a fit.

The truck had pulled up outside the main doors, which were big and dark red. The men jumped out immediately and rolled up the back. They seemed in a hurry. I suppose they wanted to make sure they could leave again before night fell. I didn't blame them. I wondered whether I could slip them some cash to let me stow away in the back when they went.

"Did we win the lottery or something?" I asked as we climbed out of the car. I was so stiff I could barely stand upright.

"This is just how they used to build the plantation homes, way back when," said Mum, as if that explained how we could afford a place like this. Or, for that matter, why we would want one even if we could.

We headed for the main door behind Dad, who didn't even knock before he went in. For a moment I thought that was weird. Then I remembered that the place belonged to us. Which was even weirder.

I wondered how long it had been since anyone had lived here. The place was silent. The floor of the big entrance hall was wood, which I guess isn't surprising, but it was perfectly polished, which was. I mean, who bothers to polish a floor that never gets walked on? There were doors and corridors leading off left and right, and a giant staircase in front of us. Halfway up it spilt in two to become the balconies of an upper level that had more doors and corridors.

We stood there, three strangers in a house that was ours, but wasn't.

"Hello?" Dad called, after a moment. "Anyone about?"

I swear you could have heard a pin drop. Then something did drop, outside – there was a *thump* as a removal man didn't quite manage to keep his grip on one of the crates. I hoped it wasn't mine, but I didn't even go to look. Neither did Mum or Dad. It felt like we'd all been absorbed into the silence of the house. My ears felt full of glue.

"Hello?" Dad called again, taking another step forwards.

A shriek echoed down from the balcony. I nearly

cacked myself. I saw Mum jump, too, and Dad. The shriek was followed by another and then the kind of manic laughter you hear if you have to walk past a first-year classroom after the bell's rung for lunch. One of the doors on the balcony opened and out came this stream of kids. There were five of them – all girls, all about ten. They charged out of the doorway, all shouting and chattering at once.

"Hey!" Dad called, over the sounds that were bouncing down the stairs like high-pitched pipe bombs. "Hello!"

The girls came to a standstill at the top of the stairs. It was like watching something out of a cartoon – the first one stopped and the others all slid into her like ducklings on a frozen pond. They stared down at us, mouths gaping. But on the plus side they had stopped shrieking, so, you know, small mercies.

Another door opened but this time there was no horrific shrieking. Instead, a guy in his twenties with mussed-up curly brown hair and glasses appeared. He was frowning.

"Girls," he said, in that tone that you know means he's said it a million times before and expects to have to say it a million more. "What have I told you about the noise?" Then he looked over the balcony and noticed us. "Ah ha!" he cried, as if we were long-lost family. "You must be the Strombergs! Welcome!"

"Hi," said Mum and Dad in unison. I didn't say anything. My head was insisting that this was all some kind of weird dream.

"These are the Strombergs, the family that has bought the forest," the guy said to the kids. "I'm Tomas," he added, which I guessed was aimed at us. "I've just got to save the report I'm working on, then I'll come down. Give me a moment?"

"Sure." Dad nodded.

Tomas stepped back into the room and then reappeared a second later. "Hey," he called. "They did tell you about the children, right?"

Mum and Dad both laughed, once again as if everything in this situation was entirely normal and not epically screwed up in any way.

"Oh, yes," said Mum, with a smile that made me realize I hadn't seen her smile, not really, in a while. "They told us about the children."

No one had told *me* about the children.

# Chapter Two

An hour later we were all sitting around a properly stoked fire in what I assume was once a ballroom or something. Now it was mostly empty apart from a long wooden table that ran down the middle and three large leather sofas arranged around a massive stone fireplace at one end of the room.

The kids – and it turned out that the group we'd seen were only a sample of the girls and boys who were in residence – were sat around the table, eating dinner from a buffet that had been laid out on another table by the wall. Well, I say they were eating dinner, but they could have been initiating World War III. How can twenty kids make so much noise? My parents and Tomas didn't seem to notice. The four of us helped ourselves to food and then we moved over to the sofas, where Mum and Dad went about getting all cosy despite the fact that our new home already seemed to be occupied.

"When the estate agent explained to us about the programme, we thought it was a wonderful idea," said my mum. She'd got her feet tucked up under one of the sofa cushions, like she used to do back at home. "How long have you been running it?"

*What programme?* I asked silently. *Can someone please tell me what the hell is going on?* I wasn't going to ask out loud, though. I still wasn't talking to my parents.

"This'll be my fifth year," Tomas said. "It's been pretty successful, I'm pleased to say. I'm from the region, and it's important to me to get kids from further afield interested in what I've been doing here." He leaned forwards, his elbows on his knees, hands clasped together, his face eager. "It might be too soon to bring this up, but do you have any thoughts about whether you'd be willing to continue letting us use the plantation? It'd be great if the programme could continue."

I shifted in my seat. Seriously, what were they on about? *What programme?*

"We've already talked about it and we'd love you to continue," said my dad as Mum nodded. "To be honest, we'll probably need the income, at least to begin with."

"Fantastic!" said Tomas, with a disturbingly wide grin. "There are so few places open to running conservation courses these days. The larger plantations don't want to know – too many legal issues involved in letting non-employees loose on their land."

Conservation. So that was it. Tomas was a tree-hugger and his purpose in life was to instil the noble art of tree-hugging into the next generation. Because, obviously, given that Sweden is only seventy per cent forest, we're really struggling to get anything going in that department. That other thirty per cent could really use a helping hand before it's too late.

"I love that you'll be continuing the family-run tradition here. Storaskogen has such a fascinating history," Tomas went on. "I've always thought someone should write a book about it. Back in the 1940s it almost went under – timber yields were too low to make it viable and it nearly ended up absorbed into one of the larger plantations. But somehow it turned a corner and it's flourished ever since, which is remarkable for such a relatively small operation. I'm sure you'll enjoy getting to know the place. I'm just sorry you've got to share your new home with these hoodlums for the next few days," he added, glancing over at the chaos vortex that was in the process of swallowing the table.

Mum smiled but it was a bit lopsided, as if someone had stapled one side of her lips to her teeth. "It's nice," she said. "Nice to have the children here, I mean."

Dad reached over and squeezed her hand as the door at the end of the room opened and an old lady tottered in carrying an empty tray. She gave us a look that suggested we smelled of boiled cabbage and then made straight for the kids' table to start clearing the plates. She looked about ninety, but she moved too fast for that, with strange little jumping tiptoe steps as if she were about to break into a run but kept thinking better of it.

"Ah – that must be Dorothea, is it?" Dad asked brightly.

"The housekeeper – yes." Tomas nodded.

"Dorothea," Dad called, standing up and making to go to her, "we haven't had a chance to meet you yet. Why don't you leave that for a bit? Come and have a drink instead, then we'll help you clear the table."

The old woman kept her back turned as she continued to pile dirty plates on to her tray. She didn't say a word.

"Dorothea?" Dad said again, a little louder this time. I guess he was assuming that she was deaf, which was a pretty fair assessment, under the circumstances. But the old woman could obviously hear perfectly well, because at that point she turned round and stared at him.

"Hi," Dad said again, with slight uncertainty. "Come and have a drink – we'd love to say hello properly."

The housekeeper looked over at the three of us still seated on the sofa. It felt a little like being stared at by one of those paintings whose eyes seem to follow you around the room. Then she turned on her heel and disappeared back through the door. It banged shut behind her. Dad came back to the sofa, a pained look crossing his face.

"Don't worry about her," Tomas told him. "She's a strange old stick, but no one knows this place better than she does – she's worked here for decades. She's stuck in her ways, but she'll get used to you."

Dad smiled and sat down again. "I'll have to

launch a charm offensive against her. I'm famous for them, aren't I, darling?"

Mum again. Not me. Just in case that wasn't clear to you by now.

"In future, I can see us going back to Stockholm when the season's over, but we'll be staying here this winter," Dad went on. "Mainly so I can go over the books and try to work out how to get the business restarted. I need to re-establish some of the sawmill contacts. I've been looking at the lay of the land and there's a large swathe of unmanaged forest in our northern sector that I want to clear over the next year."

Tomas's smile froze. He stared at Dad.

"You can't be serious," he said.

"Sorry?" Dad asked.

"That's the old-growth forest you're talking about."

Dad shrugged. "I guess it must have been there a long time, yes."

"'A long time'?" Tomas repeated with a slight edge of laughter to his voice that had nothing to do with humour. "Try thousands of years."

Tomas was annoyed, I realized. Not only

annoyed – he was angry. I sat up straighter. Things had suddenly become far more interesting.

"I've done the research," Dad said, oblivious. "It makes far more economic sense to level that section of land and plant more managed forest."

"Well," said Tomas slowly. "Yes, I suppose that's probably true – if you're a complete Neanderthal with no sense of wider ecological responsibility."

Dad opened his mouth, but at first no sound came out. His eyes bugged in surprise. "Now, hold on a—"

"Have you even seen what you're planning to cut down? Actually, don't bother to answer that, because I already know the answer. Of course you haven't. Even if you did, you wouldn't understand what you were looking at."

"Tomas…" Mum began, in her placating tone of voice, but Dad cut in before it did any good.

"I'm pretty sure I don't need to see an extra hectare or two of fir trees, however old they are, to know what they're like. Why do conservationists assume that everyone else is a complete imbecile?"

"Well, for a start, they're not fir trees," Tomas said angrily. "Which, if you had truly done any meaningful research, you would know."

"Of course I know that," Dad laughed. "Up here they'll be Scots Pine or Norway Spruce. It's a figure of speech, Tomas. They all look the same. Most people wouldn't be able to tell the difference, so what does it matter except to score some stupid self-righteous point?"

"It matters," Tomas hissed, "if the person who is supposed to be caring for this area can't tell the difference – or worse, doesn't care."

"They're all trees," Dad pointed out. "They're all trees and they're all on *my* land. Which, as you pointed out yourself, has been managed to produce timber commercially for decades."

"Excuse me," Tomas said. "I need to see to the children." Then he stood up and walked over to the kids' table, deliberately turning his back on us.

I was impressed. It usually takes longer for Dad to wind people up that badly. I got up, too.

"Well," I said, "all this excitement is too much for me. I'm going to bed. Try not to piss off any more locals, Dad, yeah? They've probably all got pitchforks and flamethrowers."

I left them there and went up to my room again. I'd only seen it for about five minutes so far, when I trailed along after the removal men with my single crate. Mum had already chosen where I was going to sleep.

"Just to begin with," she'd said. "You can move later if you want to."

It wasn't a bad room, all things considered. It was big – of course it was, everything in this crazy house was big – and it was at the back of the house. It was pretty square – in shape as well as décor, but what else could I expect? There was a huge bed with duvets and blankets layered on top of it. My plastic crate was standing in the middle of the polished wooden floor. It was blue, floating on the ocean of wood like a confused Noah's ark.

I went to the window. It was dark outside, with a fat moon and weak little stars hanging in the night sky. The trees surrounded the house, the forest starting a few metres from the back wall. They definitely looked like fir trees to me, whatever Tomas had said. They all had that triangular Christmas-tree look to them, although you'd have to have a pretty big house to fit one of these in the corner of your living room. A house like this one, in fact. I still couldn't get my head around the fact that we were supposed to be living here now. That this was supposed to be *our house*. I mean, our place in Stockholm hadn't been a shoebox either but this was something else. I wasn't sure I liked it, and that wasn't only because I was angry with my parents for disrupting my life. It was too big, too strange. It didn't feel ... right.

I stared out at the trees for a while. They were massive, all packed close together. There was a slight wind moving their spindly tops, but under that they were one dense, black mass. There was a sound, too. I thought it was the wind at first – but it was sharper than that: one single high note, rising through the trees to pierce the sky. It seemed to go on and on – more than a whistle, less than a song. It soared towards the stars and then suddenly dipped again, lower, lower, only to hike higher again.

Then the trees stopped moving. All of them.

They just ... stopped.

It must have been the wind dropping but still, it was creepy. Then I realized that the sound was still there, rising and falling. So it definitely wasn't the wind. Then it stopped, too. Everything outside my window was silent and dark. Empty. A void. A second later the fir trees started moving again, all at once, like they'd never stopped.

I tugged the curtain shut and turned my back on the window. Then I went to the bed and got in. I didn't even undress. I pulled the duvet over my head and took my phone out of my pocket.

Not a single bar. Not one.

There's a song in the trees.
They whisper rage,
whisper murder.

*It is time*, they say.
*Do you remember?*
*Do you remember what must be done?*
*Do you remember what is owed?*

# Chapter Three

My wake-up call the next morning was laughter. Not the pleasant, happy-go-lucky kind. This was the hysterical horror-film kind from something that needed to be put out of my misery. It rolled through the hallway outside my room along with the manic beat of running feet, as performed by a drummer with zero sense of rhythm. I'd just decided that I was about to be eaten by zombies when an exasperated male voice yelled something. The racket descended to a harsh whisper and I remembered the children. Then I remembered everything else. If I hadn't been seriously starving, I would have pulled the duvet over my head and gone back to sleep. Instead, I dragged myself out of bed. It's safe to say that my feelings about this move had not improved.

There was a mirror on one wall of the room, large and oblong, about the same size as me. It was pretty ancient. I think the frame had been gold once but now it looked the way an old coin does, rubbed dull. It also had those weird age spots all over the glass. Maybe once it'd had sentimental value and that's why it hadn't been thrown out, because as something to check your reflection in it was pretty useless. Not that I cared. I rarely looked at myself in the mirror and whenever I did I wished I hadn't bothered. I thought about changing my clothes, but I couldn't be bothered to do that either. It wasn't as if anyone would be able to tell the difference. Everything I wear is black or grey, or was once black and is now grey. And even if I had cared, there wasn't anyone in this *forest* to impress anyway.

Downstairs the same table was surrounded by the same mass of kids, all talking at once as they tried to stuff food into their mouths. There was no buffet this time and I stood in the doorway for a while, wondering whether the people who actually owned the house were likely to have a chance to get breakfast. Then, as it dawned on me that I didn't know where the kitchen was and that it was entirely possible I'd get properly lost if I went looking for it, Dorothea appeared. She scuttled out of a door across the other side of the hallway with that weird walk, wearing an old pea-green dress, flat shoes that may once have been brown but were now scuffed a dull white, a brown cardigan and an apron. The apron had big cheery red flowers on it. That gave me the creeps. It was as if Cruella de Vil had decided to put her hair up in bunches with pink spotty ribbon.

"You'll be wanting breakfast, I suppose," she muttered as she passed me. Then she jerked her head, which seemed to be saying that I should follow her.

Beyond the next door she opened was an oasis of calm, populated by my parents. They were sitting at a small round table covered with a white tablecloth. For a moment I had a similar feeling to the one I'd had the night before in my room: that we were in a hotel rather than somewhere that was supposed to be our home. Everything felt slightly skewed. I stood there stupidly. My parents looked up and seemed as awkward as I did.

The old woman jerked her head at the table. There was one empty place setting.

"Dorothea," my dad began as I sat down. "You really don't have to make us breakfast every day. We're very happy to do it ourselves."

Dorothea gave a half shrug but didn't say

anything. She sloped off through yet another door, appearing a few minutes later with a plate of bread rolls and some cheese and ham. She plonked them down in front of me. In his usual head-in-the-sand way, Dad seemed oblivious to the nuclear levels of hostility she was emitting and carried on speaking in a forced, cheery tone that made him sound like a totally patronizing idiot.

"So, we were wondering, Dorothea, if you could give us some information about the history of the place? I mean, you've been housekeeper here for so long, and—"

Dorothea turned her back and walked away. She was halfway to the door before her mutter made it back to the table. "Got to get the bread out of the oven."

My rolls were very definitely fresh. They were still hot, in fact, suggesting that there was nothing left in the oven to come out, but I didn't tell Dad that. He looked crestfallen. I felt bad. OK, so sometimes he can be an idiot but I have to admit that he does mean well most of the time.

"There are showers, you know," Mum said, looking me up and down.

"Good morning to you, too," I said.

"A shower every morning would probably put you in a better mood," she said.

"*I'm* the one that needs to be in a better mood?"

Dorothea appeared again, this time with coffee, which she bashed down on the table so hard I was surprised that the cafetiere didn't break. Then off she went again, with that strange fast-slow skitter, back through the door into the kitchen.

"Why is she here?" I asked.

"She lives here," Dad said. It was a useful clarification because obviously, before he'd told me that, I'd been under the impression that she teleported into the house every day from somewhere else. "She's got a bedroom in the attic."

"But why? We bought the house, not her, right? Can't we sack her or something? She gives me the creeps." Although I had to admit that her bread rolls were pretty good.

"Dorothea's lived here at Storaskogen for most of her life," Mum said, looking as annoyed as she sounded. "She doesn't have any family left and she's an old woman with nowhere else to go — we can't turn her out. I can't believe you'd even

34

suggest such an unkind thing."

"All right, all right."

"She can keep working as long as she wants to," Mum went on.

I saw Dad cast a glance at her, which she avoided. It made me think this was an argument they'd already had. It was probably one of those weird adult compromize things. Dad had won the 'let's move to the middle of nowhere and completely screw up our lives' argument and Mum had won the 'let's keep the creepy, rude old bat' argument.

"Or until she's too frail," Mum added. "Then we'll work something out. But I'm not just turning her out of her home. Who would do that?"

I opened my mouth to answer but Dad had apparently decided that it was a rhetorical question and cut in instead.

"So, Tomas and the children will be out of the house most of the day," he said. "I want you to help me take an equipment inventory, starting with the outbuildings."

I sighed. "Stocktaking? Really? Do I have to? Can't Mum do it?"

"Your mum's tired after the journey yesterday.

She needs a rest. Anyway, she wants to do the same inside the house, don't you, darling?"

Mum nodded. She was looking pretty pale and tired, I had to admit, but hey – weren't we all?

"What's the rush?" I asked. "Aren't we here for, like, ages? Can't we take a breath first?"

A familiar line furrowed between Dad's eyebrows. "I would have thought you'd like to learn more about our new home and its surroundings."

"Er, no. What I'd really like is an internet signal."

Dad sighed. "Do you have to be so difficult?"

"*I'm* the one being difficult? Because I want to be connected to the outside world, that's being difficult?"

"You could try making a bit of an effort..."

"Why should I? You brought me here. I didn't have a choice. Why do *I* have to make the effort?"

Dad said nothing. I knew I hadn't won the argument – he'd just got tired of having it.

I didn't really listen to the rest of their conversation over breakfast. I munched my way through my food, wondering what Poppy and Lars were doing at that very moment. I kept checking my phone in case it miraculously generated its own signal but of course it didn't.

I left our breakfast room as the children were preparing to head out for their morning activity. They were all in the entrance hall, making so much noise that I swear I could feel the floor juddering under my feet. As I was trying to work out how to get to the stairs without having to negotiate a mass of flailing feet and arms, Tomas waded into the centre of the maelstrom and held up his arms. The noise level dipped slightly.

"Right!" he shouted. "Let's go!"

Watching the expedition leave the house was like observing some insanely excited military operation in one-third scale. At their tutor's shout the kids all lined up in twos with their matching bright red jackets and little packed lunches. Then Tomas led them out and they all trooped through the double doors and away into the line of trees beyond.

Of course I ended up helping Dad. He has this knack for guilt-tripping. It works on everyone, so well that they usually end up going along with his plans whether they want to or not. It was another possible explanation for how we ended up at Storaskogen in the first place. If I hadn't been so mad with Mum for letting it happen, I'd probably have asked her about it. Anyway, the alternative to helping Dad seemed to be starting the homeschooling shenanigans he'd mentioned before we left Stockholm. A pile of algebra textbooks had been strategically placed in an ominous position on one of the hallway tables. After I'd seen them, stocktaking didn't seem like too bad an option after all.

There were three outbuildings: one large metal barn that looked quite new and two slightly smaller wooden structures that could have been in the same place for a hundred years, they looked so old. The newer barn had been built between the older two so that they formed a line that faced one side of the house, with their backs to the surrounding forest. Between the house and the outbuildings someone had poured gravel to make a driveway as wide as the road that led in through the plantation.

It was the newer barn that Dad marched towards. I trailed behind, wondering how my life had come to this. It was a gloomy day with heavy cloud overhead, hanging so low that the tops of the firs seemed to press right against it. Whatever sun was up there looked like I felt – as if it'd rather go back to bed and do this whole getting up and existing thing another day.

"Right," said Dad as we reached the barn doors. He thrust a clipboard towards me. "You hold that. Let's get going." He unlocked the door and dragged it open. I peered into the slatted dark inside.

"Wow," I said, despite myself.

Dad moved to stand beside me with his hands on his hips. He nodded. "There's some pretty serious stuff in here."

For once he was right. Inside the barn was a series of huge pieces of machinery that would have had engineering geeks wetting their pants. We wandered in and looked around. Everything was clearly designed for felling, stripping, slicing and dicing trees in the most efficient way possible. The biggest chunk of change was a truck-like thing with six caterpillar wheels and a mean-looking grabber on the front. The grabber was obviously detachable as there were other fittings dotted around – some that looked like giant scorpion pincers, others with large circular saws. There was also what seemed to be a portable conveyer belt with wheels and two caged trailers.

Now, I know what you're thinking. No, really

– I do, I'm smart like that. You're reading this and thinking, *Well,* dur. *You guys are on a* timber *plantation. Of course there are going to be big bits of forestry equipment all over the place. And yet you sound confused. Seriously, how dumb are you?* And I get that, I do.

But see, here's the thing. It wasn't the equipment that was weird. It was the state it was in. Because hardly any of it had been used. There was one truck with tyres that might have seen a few miles but that was it. Everything else belonged on a catwalk for seriously large machinery. That big harvester? There was shrink-wrap plastic sealed around all the levers in the cockpit. There was still a clear plastic coating on the windscreen – you know, like the sort you get on a new phone and have to peel off. There must have been over six figures' worth of shiny just-rolled-out-of-the-factory equipment standing in that barn and none of it had even been touched.

So, yeah. Bet you're not feeling quite so smug now, right?

"Where did all of this come from?" I asked Dad as he checked over one of the chainsaws. "Did you have it delivered before we got here?"

"The previous owner bought it all and then

decided to sell the plantation. Most of it's never been used – he'd only just started logging when he decided to jump ship," Dad said. "Good for us, I can tell you – I got all of this for a fraction of what it would have cost new."

I frowned. "Why did he change his mind so quickly?"

Dad shrugged. "Originally he was going to clear-cut all of the old forest to rejuvenate the young timber stock – that was what gave me the idea in the first place. Maybe he realized it was a bigger job than he'd thought and decided he couldn't devote all the time to it that it would need. His wife died of cancer a few years ago, sadly, so he was bringing up their son on his own. Doing that here would be pretty difficult even without the stresses of running the plantation. I think he's only in his thirties. Whatever the reason, he sold up and they both left."

I stared at the teeth on one of the rotary cutters. Mum gets pissed off if I buy a packet of cereal and don't finish it but this guy gets away with spunking hundreds of thousands on brand-new equipment, uses it for five minutes and then changes his mind.

There is no justice in the world.

# Chapter Four

I helped Dad out for a couple of hours, ticking off the names of equipment from his list as he foraged around in the barn and yelled out weird things like "Rottne H8". By the end of the exercise he seemed pretty happy and I'd crossed off everything on his list, so I guess that meant the absent owner hadn't pulled a fast one and nicked off with a random saw blade that Dad had paid for.

It was about midday by the time we finished. When we got back to the house Dad went off to find Mum. I decided that hanging around in his sightline might be a bad idea in case he decided I needed to be set some algebra lessons. Anyway, he'd been right about one thing – I did want to get a better look around. So far all I'd seen of the house were the central bits, the big room where the kids ate, our own dining room, and my bedroom and bathroom. Some further exploration was necessary.

Dad had headed straight up the stairs so I figured that Mum was probably going through the bedrooms. Which meant I should start downstairs, where I could avoid contact with both of them for as long as possible. I started in the corridor that led off to the left from the main staircase. It wasn't particularly wide but there were plenty of doors leading off from both sides.

All the doors were shut but none of them were locked. The first room I looked into was small and narrow, with only a huge cupboard and an empty table inside. I went in and opened the cupboard – it was full of linen, nothing else. Tablecloths, I think. They were all folded super-tidily, suggesting that someone had come along with a ruler and checked and *re*-refolded every neat little square until they were perfect. Imagine that – a whole room for table linen, all of it crisply folded – and for what? So that for a few weeks every year a bunch of messy school kids could tip their dinners all over it? I could easily imagine Dorothea standing at the table, folding sheet after sheet, muttering under her breath. What a life.

The room right next door to the linen emporium was a library. It was massive, almost as big as the room where the kids ate dinner. It was at the other end of the house and I realized that it mirrored where that room was on this side of the staircase, like some kind of architectural balance thing was going on. I wandered in, pretty stunned by the size of it. It was lined with books and had a huge fireplace set in one wall. There were little tables dotted around, too, with things like old globes on them. There must have been thousands of volumes in there, floor to ceiling, all properly leather-bound and shelved perfectly neatly as if no one had ever even read them. Or rather, as if someone went around in here tidying and dusting obsessively, which was probably more like it. At least now I knew what Dorothea did all day.

I tried to imagine what sort of person would build a room like that. It didn't feel like the kind of place where the previous owner would have spent his time. Hadn't Dad said he was in his thirties with a kid? This felt like an older person's room, the kind of older person who wouldn't go in for having a little kid running about in it. Everything felt like it belonged in a museum. I wondered how long it had been there and who it had belonged to. I also wondered why the hell it was all still there. I mean, I was pretty sure that nothing in that room had moved for a century. That's not normal, right? When you buy a house, you usually buy *just* the house, not everything in it as well. Even if you agree to buy some of the furniture, that doesn't include stuff like books, does it? Except that here it didn't seem that anything had been take out at all. It was the Dorothea thing all over again.

I went into room after room. It was the same in all of them. Nothing had been cleared. The place had been sold lock, stock and barrel, without anyone carting away the stuff that was already here. It obviously hadn't seemed weird to my parents – although as we know by now, clear thinking isn't their strong point. I can imagine my dad being really enthusiastic about the prospect of buying a house with someone else's tat left dumped in it. At least it meant he wouldn't have to furnish every room. In fact, I bet that was his exact argument to Mum. I can hear his voice saying precisely that. *Darling, it'll save such a lot of time and effort. We can concentrate on the important things.* I guess that explains why most of our stuff went into storage.

But as I thought about it, it began to seem more and more strange. There were still paintings hanging on the walls. There were more books on more bookcases. One of the rooms was a study – there was a big desk with six drawers, three on either side of the old office chair pushed into the gap in the middle. I pulled at one, expecting it to be locked, but it wasn't. It was full of papers. I tried another drawer, then another. They were all unlocked, stuffed full of things like ink pens and notebooks, grocery receipts and old, decaying elastic bands, which to me seemed completely whacko. I could understand leaving furniture where it was, maybe even paintings if you didn't want to have to deal with storing them and selling them. But personal papers?

The one thing I didn't see anywhere was photographs. This I noticed because I'd decided I wanted to see what the other people who had lived in this place were like. I mean, if Dorothea was anything to go by, we Strombergs didn't have much to look forward to. Maybe that's how everyone who lived in this neck of the woods ended up looking eventually. Maybe she was actually only forty or something. Perhaps living in the middle of nowhere prematurely sucked all the life out of you. I could believe that. So I looked around but photographs were pretty much the only things that I couldn't find. Which made a kind of sense, I suppose – photographs are about as personal as you can get if you don't care who sees your bank statements, right?

But the other thing I noticed was that there weren't any gaps for them, either – no spaces on tables or shelves where a frame might have stood, or shadows on the walls from pictures that had been removed. So it crossed my mind that maybe there hadn't been any in the first place, which also seemed a bit weird. OK, so it's not like we're the closest family ever, but even we had pictures of ourselves dotted around the old house in Stockholm. I began to actively look for photographs. I pulled open drawers and moved things around on shelves. Nothing. I went back into rooms I'd already been in, searching. Zip.

That's when I saw her. I was coming out of one room and about to go into another when the hairs stood up on the back of my neck. You know that feeling you get when you're being watched? I turned to look down the corridor and sure enough, there was Dorothea, standing in the shadows at one end with her arms hanging loosely by her sides, watching me. What freaked me out wasn't that she was watching me, exactly, but where she was while she was doing it. She was right at the end of the corridor, near the large window that was built into the end of the house. Through the window behind her I could see the dark wall of trees. To get there she would have had to walk right past the room I'd been in, so she must have heard me moving about inside. But instead of sticking her head round the door to see what I was doing like a normal person would, she had decided to walk past the door into the shadows and stand there, lurking, until I came out again.

I mean, it wasn't that she'd been passing by, heard me and then paused to see me leave.

She'd been waiting.

*Spying.*

I stared at her but she didn't move. In the end I turned and walked away, heading back to the main hallway and the stairs so I could carry on my exploration on the first floor. I felt her eyes on me every step of the way. I had this sudden, crazy urge to look over my shoulder, in case she was doing that half run, half walk of hers right at me. I imagined her moving faster than I had thought possible, scuttling full tilt down the corridor as she stared at my back with those old, watery eyes stretched wide, ready to … *to what?*

I forced myself not to turn round but it was a struggle. It was even harder not to run. But I managed it. By sheer force of will I nonchalantly went to the stairs and started walking up them, one at a time. Halfway up I glanced down but there was no sign of her. Maybe she'd had a reason to be in one of those rooms after all and she'd gone back in to do whatever it was she'd been there to do. I told myself that had to be the answer, because otherwise she'd somehow managed to hot-foot it right behind me down the corridor and across the main hallway without me either hearing or seeing her as she did it. And that wasn't something I really wanted to think about her being able to do, if I'm honest.

My heart rate didn't return to normal until I'd made it all the way up the stairs.

On the first floor, two of the big bedrooms had

been turned into dorms for the kids – ten basic camp beds set in rows in each, one for the boys and one for the girls. I didn't bother going into them as they were rooms where the original furniture had already been taken out and besides, I figured that whatever secrets they might have contained had long since been mined by fingers smaller and grubbier than mine. I didn't go into Tomas's room either, which was right in-between. Prying into stuff left behind by people who were long gone was one thing but going through his stuff, psycho tree-hugger or not – well, everyone's got to have a line, right? That was mine. I also avoided the room that I could tell my parents were in. I could hear the murmur of their voices through the door, rising and falling as I passed.

Most of the other rooms were pretty bare. Thin beds, white walls. A couple of the doors were locked and I thought about trying to break in but then I remembered Dorothea's spying and thought I'd better leave it until I knew for sure she was occupied elsewhere. Who knew where she was lurking at that moment. Anyway, there'd be plenty of time, right? All winter, apparently. Better leave some activities for later on, is what I was thinking. Besides, I peered through some of the keyholes and there didn't seem to be anything different inside the locked rooms compared to the unlocked ones – they were bedrooms, that was all. It made me think that the fact they were locked was just an oversight rather than a deliberate move to keep people out.

I did finally find a photograph and I didn't have to go through a locked door to get to it. It was lying face down in the bottom drawer of a chest in one of the disused bedrooms. It had obviously been there a while. I brushed off the dust as I picked it up and turned it over. It was big enough to hold in two hands. The picture was black and white and showed the outside of the house – I recognized the double doors easily enough. It must have been taken in summer, because there was some kind of climbing plant with big open flowers hiking its way up the walls around the entrance. Three people stood on the low steps that led up to the door – a man, a woman and a kid. The man was standing on the top step, right outside the door of the house. His arms were crossed and his chest was puffed out, as if to say, "This? Yeah, this is all mine. All your asses? Yeah, they're mine, too." You know the sort. Beside him, on the two lower steps, stood the woman and the kid, both of whom looked pretty miserable. Beyond them, in a line, stood all their servants. It didn't tell me much really, other than that it is genuinely possible to capture boredom on camera. So I put the picture back where I found it and there ended my quest.

As I headed back towards the stairs, I thought I saw something in the shadows. But when I turned my head to look, there was nothing there.

We sleep.
We curl together in the dark and dream.
Of hallways and passages. Of warmth.
Of hands, of feet.
Of voices.

*Who were we?* we ask.

*No one*, say the trees.
*Nothing. You are ours.*
*You are needed. Listen to the song.*
*Do you remember what must be done?*

We begin to.

# Chapter Five

Without the children to fill it, the house was really quiet – too quiet. It felt as if I were in one of those hermetically sealed scientific unit things, where you can only talk to the people outside via a microphone. I sat on my bed and filled my ears with Korn and Mastodon instead. I never in a million years thought I'd say this but I was relieved when the crazy tidal wave of the kids' excitement came washing back into the house. They bounced and rollicked out of the trees with as much energy as they'd had when they disappeared into them that morning. I took my earphones out and listened as the sound swelled into the building from the ground up. It filled the place as if the house was a bubble, holding all the noise inside it. I wondered whether, if I went outside right then, I'd be able to hear what was going on inside at all.

I didn't actually conduct that experiment.

The next morning I was sitting with Mum and Dad at breakfast again when Tomas appeared in the doorway. He and Dad eyed each other like suspicious dogs.

"Look," said Tomas. "I want to say that I'm sorry for the other day. I'm just … passionate about this place. That's all."

Dad looked at him steadily for a moment and then nodded. "Sure. I get that."

There was a moment of silence in which I tried not to make it look as if I was interested in hearing every word of this extremely awkward exchange. I'm pretty sure I failed, to be honest, but I don't think anyone noticed. Mum was clearly as interested as I was.

"Anyway," Tomas went on after a moment, "I'm taking the children out to the edge of the old-growth forest today. I thought you might like to come with us. See for yourself what I'm talking about."

I thought Dad was about to say a flat-out no when the tree-hugger cut in again.

"I can show you some of the most recent felling while we're at it," Tomas added. "It's out that way, too."

Mum and Dad glanced at each other. "I'm game

55

if you are," Mum said quietly. "Besides, I can give Tomas a hand with the children."

Dad's face creased into a frown as Mum looked down at her plate. "Really?" he said. "You want to do that?"

She looked up at him again. "Yes," she said, with a steely edge in her voice. "I do."

I looked from Mum to Dad and back again. Had I just missed something? Because even for my parents, that was weird. But Dad was already turning to Tomas.

"Sure," he said. "We'll join you. But don't expect me to have some huge epiphany about your trees. This place has to earn a living or it just won't survive."

Tomas gave a smile, although it wasn't difficult to see that his eyes were doing something different. "We'll be leaving in half an hour," he said. "See you then."

Tomas left, shutting the door behind him. There was a moment of silence.

"I'll come, too," I said into it.

Dad gave me a surprised look. "Wouldn't have thought a stroll in the woods would be your sort of thing, considering the sore head you've been nursing about coming here."

I shrugged. "You were the one who wanted me to show an interest," I pointed out. "Don't knock it."

Truth was, I didn't like the idea of being left in the house with only Dorothea for company. The thought of that silence filling my ears again was enough to give me the chills. I kept thinking about her following me down that hallway, too. I could hear her feet skittering over the floor, even though at the time I hadn't heard a thing. That strange half run, half walk. Remembering it was enough to make me shudder. A day in the forest had to be better than that, didn't it?

So anyway, that's how I found myself trooping out with a sorry excuse for a packed lunch stuffed into my pocket. Outside, even with the kids yelling and laughing, it was weirdly quiet. The trees were so dense that their branches absorbed all sound. Tomas led us away from the house and into the forest, my mum and dad keeping pace with him, the children straggling behind in a rough line. I ended up right at the back, trying to pretend that I wasn't really anything to do with whatever was going on. Every now and then some of the girls would turn to look at me and then whisper something to each other before dissolving into giggles. I couldn't hear them. I was busy listening to Disturbed instead. I amused myself by imagining that at any moment, some diabolical, blood-thirsty creature was going to come crashing out of the gloom beneath the trees and set about munching on their heads.

I don't really understand why people walk. And I'm not anti-exercise or anything. It's not that I spend all my free time in front of the TV or playing games on the computer. I'm more likely to be out on my board. Or I was, until I gave it away and moved to a place that didn't understand what tarmac was. But still, walking? I don't get it. Running, maybe. Ambling along like you've got all the time in the world – no. So after a while I wished I'd sucked up the freakiness of the Dorothea incident the day before and stayed in the house. The fir trees channelled us on, keeping the air cold even though there was a bit of weak sun above. I didn't like them any more than I liked the house, I'd decided. A nice fresh fir smell might be what you want hanging above the dash but trust me, when you're surrounded by it, after a while it's like you've been dunked head-first into a bottle of washing-up liquid.

No one else seemed to have an issue with any of this. The class was still chatting at high-speed like a bunch of manic chipmunks. Dad and Tomas were in full-on debate mode. My mum was walking amid a little knot of children who all seemed to be trying to impress her at once. Then eventually we came to a small clearing where the trees were nothing but blunt stumps left in the ground. Tomas broke off from his conversation with Dad and stopped, turning to hold his hands up so that the rest of us would, too. The kids clustered around him like a bunch of inquisitive meerkats.

"Right," Tomas called, once the mania had died down to a dull roar. "Notebooks and pencils out, please."

There was a mass rustling as they pulled stuff out of their backpacks. Tomas spoke above it, his voice rising over the circle of massacred trees. Despite the silence it was hard to hear what he was saying. His words started by floating up into the quiet but the noise didn't get far. It just sputtered out as if he were standing in a room kitted out with sound insulation.

As I looked around I realised it had to be because of the trees. The ones lining the clearing were so dense that nothing could escape, even noise. The sound of Tomas's voice died midway to the sky, suffocated by their thick branches.

"Remember what we learned yesterday morning, about lichens? You should still have the information sheets I gave you," Tomas was saying. "Well, today I want you to locate and sketch as many different types as you can. Work in pairs and stay where I can see you. I don't want anyone getting lost. Right? Right. Off you go, then."

It was like watching ants scatter. They all ran off like excited bugs. In fact, if there were any bugs around, I pitied them. They were probably about to get squashed by a load of tweenies.

"I thought we were going to the old-growth forest?" I said, looking around. "This doesn't look very old to me."

"You're right, it's not," said Tomas. "We've stopped here so I can show your parents the most recent felling activity in this sector and because I want the kids to see the contrast between the lichens here in the planned forest and those in the old-growth areas.

You'll be pretty amazed at the difference, I can tell you. This part of the forest is very young, but the old-growth forest is part of the taiga – the northern boreal forest, which circumnavigates the whole of the northern hemisphere. It's the largest terrestrial biome that exists anywhere on earth. Its lichens are extraordinary."

From the barely suppressed excitement in Tomas's voice, I assumed that meant we'd discover that there was far more lichen in the old-growth forest than here amid the newer planting. Even I knew that lichen was a good thing. Something to do with how much oxygen there is in the air, right? More lichen = good. Less lichen = bad. Presumably this exercise was designed to teach Dad a lesson about how valuable the old-growth forest was through the cunning medium of lichen. Clearly even after Dad's mini-lecture this morning, Tomas was still hoping to win him round. *Well, good luck with that.*

I wandered over to stand next to the damp stump of an executed fir tree, staring down at the miniature landscape that had been left by the saw that had felled it. It was rough, mountain ranges crashing together, cut out of white bark turned reddish from having been exposed to the air.

"If you look here," Tomas was saying to my mum and dad, indicating another stump that seemed to have been butchered by the same saw, "you can see some of the last felling to have taken place on the plantation. This tree was downed at least nine months ago – you can tell by the colour of the flesh."

I pressed my palm to one of the mountain ranges. It crumbled under my hand, moist and weak.

"All of the new plantings you have are Norway Spruce," Tomas explained. "It's a good general purpose wood with a lot of uses from construction to furniture. It's also relatively quick growing, which is what drives a lot of plantations to start this sort of operation. And that's fine on land that isn't already home to old-growth forests. But cutting down one to replace it with this..." Tomas shook his head. "It's obscene. Over-planting of a single species for commercial reasons in place of a diverse habitat that has existed for millennia – how can anyone imagine that's a good idea?"

Dad had crossed his arms. "You said this northern boreal forest – this taiga – covers the whole of the northern hemisphere," he pointed out. "I've got less than four hectares here. You can't tell me that taking that out is going to make that much of a difference in the long term."

Tomas turned to look at him. "The taiga is disappearing fast. Soon it'll be as endangered as the Brazilian rainforest. Every part of it matters. Every part of it deserves protection – deserves *respect*. Ancient communities that lived in this area understood that. Why can't we?"

Dad made a snorting sound in his throat. "Because we're not primitives bashing two rocks together to make a fire. And these ancient communities, where are they now? They've been replaced by progress, by modernity. It's inevitable. It's the way the world works."

Tomas glowered. "It's arrogance."

"Then I guess we'll have to agree to disagree. This place needs to make us a proper living. To do that it needs to adopt modern methods. It's too small to survive otherwise: there's too much competition."

"But the fact that Storaskogen is still family owned means that it doesn't have to mirror what the big plantation conglomerates do," Tomas protested. "Can't you see that? You can preserve the old ways.

You may be the only plantation left that still can."

Dad huffed. "Not if we want to make a living."

Tomas made an impatient gesture with his hands. "How much money does one family need?"

I could see that Dad was getting more and more riled. I was all up for settling in for the show but Mum felt the need to step in.

"Perhaps we shouldn't talk about this now," she suggested. "Let's learn what we can about our forest. Tomas has a lot he can teach us, Martin."

"Only if Martin is willing to learn," Tomas said shortly. "And anyway, it's not me you should talk to if you really want to learn about living with the forest. For that you need Dorothea. She's spent her entire life in this area, as her family has for generations. She was devastated when Erik, the previous owner, started logging the old forest. To her it's like a family member dying every time one of those ancient trees is cut down."

Dad had crossed his arms and turned away. Mum smiled at Tomas.

"Well, we're here now," she pointed out calmly. "So why don't you tell us what you can?"

Tomas glanced at Dad, clearly thinking about

launching another volley. Then he gave Mum a weak smile and a nod. "All right," he said.

Storm averted. Boredom resumed. I brushed my palm against the leg of my jeans. The residue of the wood from my hand left a soft whitish trail against the black denim. Tomas started speaking again, something about the exponential increase in sales of our type of tree in the past decade. I looked around the clearing, wondering how much money the felled trees from this small part of the forest would have fetched on the open market. I could have asked, but that might have looked as if I cared.

The kids were all hard at work. Some of them were taking sneaky bites of whatever snacks they'd brought with them but, other than that, there didn't seem to be any mucking about whatsoever. I wondered what Lars and Poppy would have said about this whole thing. I took my phone out of my pocket – still no signal. Maybe I'd use the landline to phone them later. But I probably wouldn't bother. I didn't want to be the one calling, for a start. I wanted people in Stockholm to notice I'd gone without me having to point it out. Or worse, making them think that I was missing them. Way to become a sad twonk to your friends. And given that there was absolutely no way we'd be lasting at this timber lark longer than a few months, I didn't want to go back to a fanfare of humiliation. Well, no more than I'd get already, in any case.

I wandered off, staring at more stumps, thinking of more questions that I had no intention of asking. In spite of himself, Dad seemed to be engrossed in what Tomas had to say, probably because it had to do with money. Tomas was now interspersing his speech with gestures that made him look even more unbalanced, but at least they didn't seem about to kill each other.

I found myself staring into the trees. The longer I looked, the more everything else faded away. Right then I kind of liked the idea of being absorbed into nothingness. Let's face it, moving up here had pretty much sealed my fate in that regard anyway. So I went for a stroll of my own, right out of the clearing and into the trees.

# Chapter Six

It wasn't until I'd stepped out of the clearing that I realized something. On the way here, I'd assumed we were tramping along through the forest. But actually we'd been on a path. Not much of one, obviously, which is why I hadn't noticed it in the first place. But I saw that it had definitely been a path, because now I was properly inside the forest. And I'm telling you, there was a difference.

For a start, the ground was springy. There was a thick layer – several layers, in fact – of pine needles coating the ground under the firs. I'd read about that somewhere before. Don't ask me where. I'd always kind of assumed that it would be … nice. Not that I spent time specifically thinking about it, obviously. I just mean that it had got into my brain the way those kinds of things do. Anyway, walking on springy ground does sound like fun, doesn't it?

Well, it isn't. It's weird. For a start, the ground was

really uneven, because without anyone treading on it regularly, the needles pile up in − well, piles − all over the damn place. I guess when it rains or snows they get compressed a bit, but not much, so the ground is lumpy, which makes it a pain in the ass to walk on.

The second thing is that it's not a good sensation. It's unsettling, a bit like walking on the deck of a boat in rough water. Our little human brains are set to think that the ground should be level and solid. The springiness throws you off-balance. As I walked, I didn't find myself thinking, *Hey, this would be a really cool place to settle down for a nap − a nice, comfortable bed of pine needles.* I thought, *This is seriously odd.*

The reason, I worked out pretty quickly, that there were so many pine needles on the ground was that most of the lower branches of the firs had shrivelled up. The bark on the trees looked like the scales of some prehistoric creature that had survived the ice age, like an armadillo, or something − it was all dry and cracked and overlapping. Out of it stuck hundreds of narrow, twiggy branches. They started right at ground level, reaching out like skeletal fingers, all dry and brittle, ready to gouge your eyes out or slash your legs if they got a chance. They looked dead but the trees themselves were alive – above my head there were plenty of branches that still had pine needles on them, green and spiky and doing perfectly well, thanks very much. So I figured the lower branches had died because it was so dark down there where I was. Leaves are there to convert the light into nutrients the tree needs, right? Well, there was hardly any to be had at ground level in that forest. It was dim and gloomy so I guess keeping those branches alive was pointless.

Trees, man. Turns out they can let little bits of themselves *die*. The bits that aren't worth keeping alive. Tell me *that* isn't creepy.

The noise inside the forest was even stranger. The firs were all planted close together in strictly regimented lines. They had grown really tall, which meant that their tops – where the branches were still alive – were high enough to be in the wind. So there was this constant rushing noise. It sounded loud yet far away, as if it were blowing a gale way up there. But where I was standing there wasn't even the hint of a breeze. It was as if I was inside a bottle, and the noise and movement all started at the open neck of the bottle, several metres above my head. Way up there where I could never reach, the treetops were constantly moving, doing stuff, being … alive.

Anyway I was standing there, getting a crick in my neck from looking up at those crazy, waving branches, when something moved in the corner of my eye. I jerked round but whatever it was had stopped. I listened but all I could hear was the *whoo-ooosh* of the wind.

I thought maybe it was a rabbit or a deer. I wandered along the two lines of trees I was standing between, the *whoo-ooosh* of the wind still going on above me. Ahead I spotted light. I headed for this little trickle of glowing sun, thinking that maybe it was another clearing like the one I'd left. But when I reached it, I saw that what had made the space to let in the light was a stream. It cut right through the stands of trees, so overgrown with rough grass that I almost stepped right into it. It was what was beyond the stream that stopped me short, though.

On the other side of the water the forest was different. It was still a dense mass of trees, but they were wilder and not as tall. There weren't only fir trees – or pine or spruce or whatever it was I was standing under right then – either. I could see other species mixed in, too. They all had different types of needles and cones. Some were silvery, as if they had been sprinkled with sugar or ice. Others were such a dark, deep green that from where I was standing, they looked black. Then there were trees that had no branches until halfway up their trunks and others that had branches as thick as my arm, with pine cones the size of a clenched fist. The trunks of some were bent and twisted. In places they were so close together that it was hard to tell where one ended and another began, but elsewhere there were wide gaps where the light reached the ground. There was absolutely no plan to how these trees had grown. No human had come along with a bunch of neat little identical mini-trees in a backpack and used a ruler to make sure they were spaced just so before dropping them in a perfect line. In fact, it didn't feel like humans had had anything to do with this place at all. Like, ever. These trees had just grown in any old way they wanted to. Naturally, I suppose you could say.

Also, instead of the ground being a compacted mulch of old brown pine needles and nothing else, there were other plants here as well – hundreds of them, grasses and bushes of all sorts. In-between were super-sized varieties of moss and everything was growing beside each other so closely that I couldn't see any bare earth at all. It was like looking at a shade palette for green paint. There were so many different hues of the same colour – in the trees, in the moss, in the lichen. Oh, and I could totally see what Tomas meant about that. Back in the clearing in the new forest, any lichen there was grew in little tufts no more than a centimetre high and you had to really search for it. Here it hung from gnarled branches in long, floaty green tendrils that didn't even look real, as if some weirdo had come along and draped strips of green gauze over everything. Every leaf, frond and branch glistened with moisture. Even the smell in the air was different. It was older, somehow. Not rotten, I don't mean that. It just seemed to hold a memory of a time when the whole world must have been like this – untouched, unvisited, unknown. Unseen by scruffy loser teenagers like me. It was like nothing I'd ever seen before. It was strange. It was creepy. It was kind of beautiful.

I looked at the trees in front of me and I thought, *Now I understand.*

When Tomas had talked about the old-growth forest, it hadn't really meant anything to me. But now, seeing it for what it was, I got it. I'm not saying I'd had that epiphany that Dad had sworn he wouldn't have himself, but I *got* it. This wasn't like the forest I'd just walked through. This was old – ancient, even.

It felt different. It wasn't only a different world. It felt like a different planet.

I don't know how long I stared across that stream. I must have been kind of mesmerized. When I finally stepped over it, my foot landed on a bushy patch of damp grass that was way closer to the edge than I'd thought. It gave way and I slipped, my arms flailing as I tried to stop myself ending up in the water. I stumbled forwards, landing on my knees. My feet splashed into the water but at least I managed to avoid a full dip in the stream.

As I got up I found myself facing the part of the forest that I'd just left. The trees stood there, all lined up, perfectly straight and incredibly tall, dense triangles packed together. For a second I couldn't see through the darkness between their dead lower branches. I could have been looking at a solid wall that I was never going to find an opening in again; as if the trees had sealed themselves behind me and had no intention of ever letting me back in. I blinked and my eyes focused – instead of a solid mass, I could see the tree trunks leading in dim but straight avenues back the way I had come. I could even see the patch of light that I knew was where my parents, Tomas and the manic munchkins were. It seemed a million miles away.

I heard a noise behind me, somewhere deep in that haphazard tangle of branches, leaves and bark. The sound of the wind had lessened. In fact, unlike in the planned forest, I could feel a breeze. It buffeted past me as I turned, ruffling my hair.

I heard the noise again and this time I saw a movement, too, something somewhere ahead of me amid the tangle. I stood really still until it shifted again. Then I walked towards it, picking my way over fallen branches and trying not to crush the moss. I got my phone out of my pocket as I went, thinking I could take a picture of whatever it was foraging way out here in the middle of nowhere.

But it wasn't a creature. It was a tree. A really big one. And it was dying.

The tree was falling over in ultra-slow motion. The others all around it were crowding in, holding it up. Every time the wind blew, the tree fell a fraction more and this huge black hole yawned open beneath it where its roots had been buried in the soil. But its neighbours refused to let it fall. They leaned against it, propping it up, determined to keep it alive. Meanwhile, its severed roots dangled in the air, hanging loosely as if they were human intestines spilling out of a slashed gut. Half were still buried in soil but the other half lifted further up out of the earth with every fresh billow of wind, creating the entrance to some unspeakable place that no one in their right mind would ever even want to look at, let alone visit. With every gust, the wind pushed at the tree, that hole opened a little wider and the tree died a little more.

I'll be honest, it wasn't the most calming thing I've ever seen. I think I knew right then that this place, this old forest, was nowhere any human had any right to be.

Another gust of wind rocked at the tree. That mouth screamed open – a big, black hole of nothing leading to nowhere.

I turned my back on it. One of the kids was crouching right behind me, his back against another tree trunk. I nearly jumped out of my freaking skin.

"*Crap*," I yelled. Then I crawled back inside my body and added, "Where the hell did you come from?"

The kid didn't answer or even look up at me. He sat with his knees pulled up to his chin and his arms wrapped round his elbows. I didn't remember seeing him before but then children all look the same to me and anyway, I was used to them travelling in rabid packs. This one seemed to have taken off his jacket and was shivering a bit. He looked a bit brown, too – clothing-wise, I mean. Brown shoes, brown trousers, cream shirt. Not very on-trend, I think is what occurred to me first, but then who gives a damn about that stuff? I, personally, am fashion-resistant. I was born this way.

"You're not supposed to be here," I told him. "I heard Tomas tell you to stay in the clearing."

The kid still didn't answer me. I would say that was a bit annoying but if I did, I'm sure you'd say something like, "Pot, kettle, black". So screw you. I won't.

"Well, don't be long," I said, a bit lamely and a bit too much like my mum. "And don't wander off," I added, which was too much like my dad. I guess I'm at that stage where it's becoming hideously apparent that we all turn into our parents. Which is one of life's many truly horrific inevitabilities.

I wondered what to do about the sulky kid and then decided I didn't have to do squat. I could still see the clearing from where we were. The kid couldn't be so dumb that he'd get lost playing hide-and-seek or whatever it was he and his mates were doing. And anyway, it wasn't my problem if Tomas was too busy hugging trees to look after his students, was it? That was his job, not mine. And besides, I really didn't want to hang around there any longer than I had to.

Then I saw what was beyond the tree the kid had been crouching against. Although I guess that you'd have to say that, actually, there was nothing to see.

The kid's tree was the last before the forest fell into a yawning blank space. A strip of trees the width of a football field had been hacked out. And I know, I know – that shouldn't really be surprising, should it? Not in a timber plantation. Not when I'd seen that clearing that Tomas had taken us to, which was pretty much the same thing.

Except that this was definitely different. This was ... *brutal*. No nice soft pine needles here. No grasses, either, or even any moss. Erik – and it had to have been him, this had to be the start of the clear-cutting of the old forest that Tomas had told us about – hadn't even left any stumps in the ground. Everything had been torn out by the roots, the ground scraped over to show the bare earth beneath. Why? To make sure it couldn't grow back, I suppose. It meant that the earth was pitted with craters. There were great big ragged holes gouged everywhere.

Erik hadn't even taken all the dead trees away. A lot were still lying here and there, some with their branches hacked off. This will sound crazy but for a second it was almost like looking at people. Lying there broken and damaged, like the victims of a bombing. All around the edge of this huge dead gap, the trees that were still standing looked like shocked families, holding on to each other, bent over with grief.

I flailed backwards. As I turned, I found myself facing the dying tree, the one that the other trees around it were trying to hold steady. It didn't want to die. They didn't want it to die. *Not another one. Not another one. Not another...*

I tried to breathe and couldn't because there was something spreading in my chest, something too huge and horrifying to navigate. I stumbled back the way I'd come. As I went I heard that sound again, that weird, singing note I'd heard on the night we'd arrived. It sounded a long way away, as if it were coming from another world.

We have been far away,
where the trees never end,
where the world is black
with night and shadow,
where the snow is forever,
but now ...

... now we are coming back.

# Chapter Seven

I jumped over the water and ran back to the clearing, my heart still hammering. No one had noticed I'd gone anywhere, which was no surprise. I must have been gone for a bit longer than I'd thought, too, because Tomas was marshalling the troops. Mum was surrounded by munchkins. Dad was examining tree trunks, probably convinced that Tomas's company had made him an authority already.

I looked around, feeling as if I'd stepped out of a parallel universe. Had any of that really happened at all? I looked down at my feet. They were still wet from my tumble in the stream. I was cold. Really cold, inside and out, and not just because of the temperature.

I knew right then that there would never be a time when I didn't hate Storaskogen.

"Right," said Tomas, over the hubbub of the children. "Now we're going to move on to the old-growth forest. Remember what I've said before – be careful where you tread, and—"

One of the kids shrieked. Then another. The next minute they were all squealing and shouting and pointing. For a moment I couldn't work out what the fuss was about. Then I saw it. Snow. Huge white snowflakes were plummeting silently out of the thick grey sky. It wasn't one or two, either. Suddenly the air was full of the stuff. I could feel it landing on my hair and sliding coldly down my neck.

I'm no expert but I was pretty sure it was too early for snow, even up here.

Tomas tried to maintain order as the assembly of kids became a miniature mosh-pit. "All right, all right!" he shouted. "I think we'll have to cut this expedition short. Let's get ready to head back to the house!"

It took a good deal more yelling to get them back into their pairs again. Then Tomas went to the head of the column and led them all out of the clearing. I looked around, wondering whether the kid that had been communing with the screaming tree had come back to the group, but I couldn't see him. I thought again about whether to tell Tomas, but I admit there was a tiny part of me that wanted to stick it to him. If the tree-hugger got all the way back without realizing that one of the tinies was missing, I figured that'd pretty much do it for his annoying Mr Moral High Ground image.

We wound back through the forest on the path that almost wasn't and the snow kept on falling. The daylight seemed to leech away until we were walking through an inky blue-blackness edged by the endless trees. I kept thinking about what I'd seen in the old-growth forest. Every time I did, my chest felt heavy, an invisible weight pressing on it.

*They're just trees,* I told myself. *What are you so freaked out about?*

At one point I stopped and looked back. The shadows seemed to be pouring out from beneath the firs, pooling in the space that made the path, except that now it was almost impossible to tell where the shadows ended and the trees began. The darkness blended into one dim blur of anti-matter that was swallowing everything. I looked up and through the gloom I saw that the tops of the trees were still. Maybe the coming of the snow had made the wind drop. But the thing was, I could still hear the sound the trees had made as the wind had moved them. *Whoo-oosh. Whoo-oosh.* It was still there, even though the wind wasn't. For a tiny second, it sounded like words. Like voices, talking low enough that I couldn't quite make out what they were saying. And there, behind the whispers, was that other sound rising again, the one I had heard as I'd left the damaged old forest. That weird, haunting, lilting song. Was it a hunting horn? If it was, who was hunting? *What* were they hunting? There was nothing out here but trees.

The whispering grew louder as that noise went on and on. There was something massive about it all, something huge that I couldn't get my head around. I was colder than I had ever been in my life. I could feel my breath in my throat like ice.

I turned round again. Of course, no one had noticed that I'd stopped. The group had got far enough ahead of me that I could only just make them out. For a second there, I almost panicked. I had a sudden image of myself from the outside, this tiny, puny human surrounded by a dense, dark forest that stretched on for God knows how far. From where I stood right then, the whole rest of the world could have become forest and I'd never

85

know because I'd been swallowed by it. I could have been the only person left alive and how would I ever know? How would I ever find anyone, any*thing* else other than trees?

In that second the song stopped but the whispering sound became louder still. I stuffed my hands in my pockets and I ran. I ran down the barely there path and I didn't look back. The snow was still falling and the flakes were bigger now, fatter. By the time I caught up with the queue of kids, there was a thin layer coating the path beneath our feet.

After that first bout of excitement, the children seemed to have quietened down. Maybe they were tired. And weirdly, I was disappointed. I wanted them to be noisy. I wanted them to be the noisiest they had ever been in the whole of their little lives to drown out what was behind me. To chase away that darkness I had felt swarming around us, towards us.

It wasn't until we got back to the house that I remembered about that one kid. I felt really bad – hell, if I'd felt that freaked out back there, what state must he be in? But then I saw that Tomas was doing a headcount. I couldn't see the boy but there was no wailing and gnashing of teeth at the end of the exercise, so he must have been there somewhere. I just hadn't spotted him, which wasn't very surprising as when they had their red jackets on they really *were* all the same.

We trooped inside the house and shook the snow off our clothes and hair. I felt better once there were walls between me and everything out there. I mean, there was a reason people starting building shelters way back when, right? Shut the door, be safe, forget what's outside. I could go with that.

"All right," Tomas called. "I want everyone to go into the dining room and sit quietly at the table. I'll see if I can get Dorothea to rustle up some hot chocolate, OK?"

There was a general running and shoving and squealing, which was less appealing than it would have been ten minutes previously.

"Do you think it's going to lay?" Mum was asking, a little anxiously. She, Tomas and Dad were gathered around one of the windows.

Tomas nodded slowly. "I think it might. One thing's for sure – I think we should cut this course short. I'll call the coach and make sure it's here to pick us up as soon as it can."

"Oh – really?" Mum sounded disappointed. "You don't – you don't want to see if it does blow over?"

"I don't think this is going to blow over," said Tomas. His voice had an ominous tone to it that I couldn't quite work out.

"Isn't it early?" Dad asked. "I thought, even this far north…"

"Yes, it's early," Tomas said, still staring out of the window to where the trees were slowly being turned white. "I've never known it this early before. It makes me think…" He stopped and clamped his lips shut as if he hadn't meant to say anything at all.

"It makes you think what?" Mum prompted, with a frown.

Tomas shook his head and then, after another pause, said, "It makes me think … it's a warning."

"A warning?" Dad repeated. "What do you mean, a warning?"

Tomas turned to look at him. "Put it this way. You won't be able to log in the snow, will you?"

Dad stared at him blankly. Then he laughed. "You're not serious? You think that – what? This is a warning from nature itself? I've never heard anything so utterly ridiculous in my life!"

Tomas turned away with a shrug. "You said that, not me."

"It's what you meant though, isn't it?" Dad said. I could tell from his tone that he was partly amused but with one foot firmly on the road to being truly pissed off. "More mumbo-jumbo meant to scare the idiots from the south, right? Well, it won't work. You hear me? It won't work."

Tomas shrugged. "Fine. But if I were you, I'd leave, too. Being stuck here without being properly prepared for a long winter is a bad idea."

"What makes you think we're unprepared?" Dad asked.

Tomas gave him a look. "Suit yourself," he said. "But I've got to get these kids out of here. I can't risk having them snowed in."

He walked away.

"I'll miss the children," Mum said, to no one in particular.

The usual pandemonium echoed towards us from the dining room. I wondered what the house would be like without it and for once I thought I understood my mum perfectly.

# Chapter Eight

That evening, the kids all stayed in their dining room. Tomas let them bring their duvets and pillows down from their rooms and gather around the big fire with more mugs of hot chocolate. I went in and sat on the sofa, not because I particularly wanted to be with everyone else but because I didn't want to be upstairs by myself. Besides, it was warm in that room with the blazing fire and the mass of bodies, and even that many hours later I was still cold. I was kind of hoping I could put on the one single TV that this place had, which – because life is cruel and adults are stupid – was also in that room. But I soon realized that there was no way I'd be able to hear it and I also suspected that there would be nothing on worth watching anyway. So I pretended to be engrossed with something on my phone as I tried to ignore everything around me.

I tuned back in when I heard a collective gasp

from the kids. Mum was sitting on the sofa opposite me, listening to the children with a smile on her face. Dad and Tomas were at the dining table, quietly going over what looked like plans of the forest.

"...and that's when he saw it," said one of the boys, in a loud whisper. He lifted both his arms up and wiggled his fingers. "It was hanging over the stairs like a cloud but it had a face! And do you know whose face it had?"

"Miriam's!" one of the girls squeaked and then clapped a hand over her mouth.

"Yup," confirmed the boy. "There was his dead wife, come back to haunt him. She reached out with arms like this—" He turned his hands into claws. "And Old Jacob fell over and had a heart attack there and then." The boy dropped his arms with a flourish. "And do you know what they found when they opened up her grave to put him in with her? Her arms were raised against the sides of the coffin. Like the body had moved ... *after* it was *dead*."

A ripple of horror passed around the crowd of kids. The storyteller grinned, satisfied. *He'll go far, that one*, I thought. I could see four years at drama school in his future and then he'd land himself a job as a giant puppet on children's TV.

There was a bit of a pause and then another of the children started telling a story. Yes, right there, in that creepy old house in the middle of a freak snowstorm, the munchkins had decided to trade ghost stories. I didn't envy Tomas – no matter how lame what they came up with would be, there was bound to be a nightmare or two later. Still, Mum didn't seem to be that bothered – she was still watching them with the same vague smile – so who was I to care? Honestly, there are times that I think I'm the only sensible person in my family and that's saying something.

A little while later – by this time I had tuned out again, bored – the door of the room opened and Dorothea shuffled in with a tray. She did her weird insectoid walk-run right across the room to where the children were sitting on the floor and started gathering up mugs.

It was one of the girls doing the storytelling this time. She was one of the quieter ones – obviously not too sure of herself. She was sitting on her duvet on the floor with her arms wrapped round her knees and her voice was trembling a bit as she spoke. She wasn't really capturing the attention of the rest of the children, who were fidgeting and whispering to each other. I felt sorry for her, in fact. I know what it's like to be that kid. There's one in every class – one that doesn't quite fit in, one that's interested in stuff that no one else cares about. They'll forever be on the edge of things, wanting so much to dive into the middle and yet always regretting it when they do.

Dorothea shuffled around as this girl spoke, not really helping matters by catching up empty mugs and slamming them on the tray with a series of clatters that almost drowned out the girl's story completely. I saw Mum frown and wondered if she was going to say something but she didn't. She let the girl struggle on.

"...anyway, the next night there was a f-f-ull m-moon," said the kid, and it occurred to me that she was telling a werewolf story. Which, I'll be honest, lessened my sympathy for her a bit. I mean, werewolves, come on. They're almost as passé as vampires, right? "And Augusta stood by the w-window. She thought s-she was safe, because how c-could Obediah get in? B-but—"

*Bang!* Dorothea slammed the full tray down on

the table, muffling whatever Obediah was about to do to Augusta with a rattle of dirty mugs. Everyone jumped. The girl who had been speaking gulped and stared up at the old woman with huge, scared eyes.

Mum straightened up with a frown. "Dorothea?" she asked. "Are you all right?"

True to form, Dorothea ignored her. She was too focused on the children. She loomed towards them, all spindle and sharpness – elbows pointing outwards, shoulders tensed, fingers spread in a far scarier version of what we'd seen drama-school boy do earlier. In fact, if she came at you out of the dark looking like that, you really might have a heart attack. The room was silent save for the crackle of the fire. All the children had frozen, as if someone had stopped time and them with it. They watched the housekeeper approach as if fearful of what she was about to do. I didn't blame them.

"What do you children know of horror?" she asked, the rasp of her voice loud in the quiet room. "Tucked up in your safe, soft little homes with your safe, soft parents and your safe, soft toys."

"Dorothea," my mum cautioned, "really, I don't think—"

94

"This forest," the old woman said roughly, speaking right over Mum, "this forest has been here forever. It is older than anything you can imagine. There are things in it you will never understand. We live in it, but we are not part of it. People go out there and they don't come back. You see? People go missing in this forest all the time. They always have. They always will. Did you know that? Consider that, the next time you go out there running and jumping and stomping about thinking you own the place. *People go missing all the time.* One minute they're there and the next they're gone. They walk into the trees and they never come out again. Next time – *next time* – that could be any one of you."

By now she was standing right over the cowering children, her fingers curled into claws ready to pounce.

"Dorothea!" My mum's angry shout took me by surprise. She was standing now. "Stop it. You're scaring them."

The old woman turned to my mum with a look of pure hate on her face. I guess she'd spent so much time up here alone, she wasn't used to being told what to do, even by people who were paying her wages.

"You. Mollycoddling them. Making them soft. Making them useless," Dorothea spat. "Useless for life. What sort of mother are you?"

"Get out," said my mum, shaking with rage. "Get out of here, now."

Dorothea stared her down for another minute. Then she smiled, her upper lip curling into an expression so vile that I think I actually shivered. The old woman walked right up to Mum, until they were almost nose-to-nose.

"The snow has started," she said, in a whisper that cut through the room clear enough for everyone to hear it. "The varulv are coming. They get closer every day."

Then she turned and left the room, moving in that horrible half walk, half run, out through the door without another word. No one went after her. No one called, or shouted or told her to stop. The rest of us were all completely silent, too shocked to even move, I think.

"That's it," said Dad, after a moment. "She's going. I don't care if she has nowhere else to live. Ingrid – are you all right?"

He went to Mum, who was still standing frozen

in the middle of the floor. As he reached her he put out a hand to touch her arm but she shook him off.

"I'm fine," she said quickly. Her voice came out too high. She cleared her throat. When she spoke next her voice was calmer but she spoke fast. "What was she talking about? The varulv? What did she mean?"

Tomas came over from behind the table. "It's a local word for wolf," he said. "But there's no need to worry. A few come from the far north in the winter but there aren't nearly as many as there used to be. You might see a few in the plantations but they stay away from humans. It's the classic story – they're more afraid of you than you are of them. Dorothea's just trying to scare you. They won't come near the house."

Mum didn't say anything. She moved further away from Dad, instead. "I'm tired," she said, and this time her voice sounded dull and distant. "I'm going to bed."

I watched her leave the room. I could see that her hands were shaking. I hoped it was because she was still angry with Dorothea but I had a feeling it was something else. She couldn't be afraid. I'd never seen my mother afraid of anything. If it wasn't fear and it wasn't anger that was making her shake, then what was it?

I didn't really want to think about that.

Tomas went over to Dad. "Winters here really are very harsh, you know," he said. "It's why I only bring the school groups here in summer and why I want to get them out as quickly as possible now. I honestly think you should consider heading out, too."

Dad tore his gaze away from the door that my mum had vanished through. He looked at Tomas as if he'd spoken in a different language.

"This is our home," he said flatly. "We're not going anywhere."

Tomas looked at him for another moment and then nodded. Then he turned to the kids with a bright smile. "Right, I've got a special treat for you tonight, something I've been saving," he said with a cheerfulness that was clearly forced. "Who's up for *Iron Man*?"

There was a chorus of yeses, although they were pretty subdued. I knew how they felt.

The trees whisper;
endlessly they whisper.
*Hurry*, they say.
*You are needed.*

But we are lost.
We have been lost for a long time.

*Who are we?* we ask.

*Listen to the song*, whisper the trees.
*Listen.*

# Chapter Nine

The snow wasn't just a flurry. It carried on all evening and through the night. When I woke up in the morning, there was a thick white layer over everything. I opened my eyes so early that it was pretty much still the middle of the night. I could tell, without even looking out of the window, that the snow was there. The house felt pensive, as if it were waiting for something. It felt, for a minute or two, like I was the only person *in* that house, as if there were nothing else here except silence and space. Even when I flicked on my beside lamp, the light seemed thin and barely there.

I looked at my phone. It was only just 5 a.m. I don't think anyone else was awake, but I already knew there was no way I was going to get back to sleep, so I got up. I didn't put the main light on. Instead, I picked my way across the floor, avoiding the crate that I still hadn't unpacked or even bothered to move, and made for the window. Pulling back the curtain, I could see five centimetres of snow on the window ledge. For a while, I didn't look further than that layer of white on the other side of the glass.

It's going to sound crazy but it took me some time to pluck up the guts to look at the forest. Stupid, right? But there was something about that silence that had filled my head, made me afraid – of what, I wasn't even sure. I just kept thinking about what it had been like to be out there among the trees and right then the fact that I was safe indoors didn't make me feel any better at all.

When I did look up, the trees were a black mass, so thick that at first I couldn't see anything but the darkness. After a few seconds my eyes began to adjust and it became easier. I could see no stars and then stars, which showed where their tops finished. I could also see that it was no longer snowing. Then, as I stood there peering out, I began to see the white.

It outlined the trees as though they'd been drawn in chalk on a dark surface. The snow made their tops seem even more jagged than I'd noticed the day before. It was almost like a kid's drawing of a Christmas tree – triangles upon triangles, sharp, simple lines at an angle to the ground.

Every tree was completely still. They stood there like a line of soldiers at attention, shoulder to shoulder, so close together that there was no space between them at all. Their heads were still and straight with their chins up. They were staring at the house. I don't know why I thought that. They could have just as easily been facing away from it. I could have been looking at their backs. But I wasn't. They were facing me, looking at *me*, one tiny figure standing in front of all those trees and the house I was in might as well not have been there at all.

*People go missing in this forest all the time…*

I thought about that tangle of ancient woodland I'd found myself in the day before. I thought about that horrible scar in the middle of it, the way the trees around its edge seemed to be in mourning. I thought about that dying tree, how the others around it seemed to be holding it up, protecting it. Scratching at the back of my mind, I heard those whispers again, the ones that had chased me back here as if they were made by something alive and angry. I heard that other sound again, too, piercing and haunting and hunting. Hunting what, though?

Hunting *what*?

I looked and I looked and I looked. As I did I felt that I was fading away into that darkness between the firs.

Then the children woke up.

Now let's all take a moment here to hail the all-conquering power of *Iron Man*. Unlike me, they obviously hadn't had any trouble at all putting Dorothea's nastiness of the previous evening out of their tiny minds. I knew this because their vocal hysteria at the sight of proper snow was probably audible from space. It woke the house – I don't only mean Mum and Dad and Tomas and Dorothea, although they probably didn't get any sleep after the first munchkin shrieked, either.

I blinked. I moved. Suddenly the gluey feeling in my ears was gone. I had the sensation that the house had moved, too, like a dog waking up and shaking itself. I looked down at my phone again. It was after 7 a.m. I'd been standing at that window staring out at the forest for two hours.

Downstairs, with the sun a little higher in the sky, the snow didn't look as bad as it had in the dark. Probably just as well, because I think Tomas would have had a heart attack if it had. He stood with my parents on the steps outside the double doors. I went out to see what they were talking about. As I crunched into the snow with my boots it hardly even reached over the treads.

"The coach will be here tomorrow," Tomas said. "As long as we don't get any more snow today and as long as the temperature doesn't drop too drastically tonight, we should be fine to get away."

"That's good," said my mum, sounding anything but happy about it. "I saw the local forecast this morning and it didn't say there would be any more."

"They didn't predict this, either," Tomas said, with the same ominous tone he'd adopted yesterday.

"Look, there's no need to worry," said my dad, in his brisk 'I can solve everything' voice. "If there is more snowfall, we can tell the coach to wait at the main road. They're sure to have cleared that, at least. Even if it snows another ten centimetres our 4x4 will make it that far. We can fit six of the kids in at a time." He clapped the tree-hugger on the back and grinned. "We'll make sure you escape this evil we heathen southerners have brought, Tomas, don't worry."

Tomas didn't smile, but then Dad's joke wasn't that funny.

I wondered how much petrol Dad had and whether he'd thought about that before making his offer. I was willing to bet that it hadn't occurred to him that, even if the kids got away, we'd better have a damn fine plan for getting out ourselves unless we were ready to be stuck here permanently. But I reckon he was convinced that the snow was going to disappear in a day or two and that by the end of the week he'd be sitting cosily in our ridiculously big and empty house, gloating at how pathetically stupid Tomas had been to get so worked up.

I didn't contribute to the conversation. They hadn't listened to me when I'd said coming here was an insane idea, so they clearly weren't going to listen if I told them I thought we should leave while we still could. Anyway, what did I know? Maybe Dad *was* right and Tomas *was* the idiot in this situation. Stranger things have happened.

No, I didn't really think so, either.

The firs were moving again. Thick globs of snow teetered on the ends of their branches and then slid slowly off as the wind moved them. They hit the ground with a soft whumping noise, one after the other. *Whhhump-whhhump-whhhump.*

I stuck my hands in my pockets and went back inside in search of breakfast.

# Chapter Ten

I'd kind of hoped the hysteria would die down after breakfast. It didn't. The snow had got into the kids' brains, turning them into zombies. The kind of zombies that could do nothing but run about, chasing each other and shrieking. Which, come to think of it, would probably mean they would be fairly harmless as actual zombies. As children, it made them pretty nightmarish.

I did my best to shut it all out. I stayed in my room as the kids ran riot. They kept begging Tomas to let them go out in the snow but he wouldn't. He was worried about them hurting themselves, I guess. Anyway, that forced them to come up with new and unusual ways of entertaining themselves, which seemed to mean making everyone else's lives a misery by doing whatever it was as loudly as possible.

I distracted myself by finally emptying out my

crate of stuff. I was in the middle of this when something cut through my haze of misery. It was *the* sound – the one I'd been hearing since we got here, that creepy, lilting call like a hunting horn. I looked up from whatever I had in my hands and listened. This time was different. This time it was coming from inside the house. Not only that, it wasn't a horn at all; I was pretty sure it was a voice.

I went to my bedroom door and opened it, listening. I could still hear it even over the sound of the kids playing. It stopped and started. Sometimes it sounded as though it was more than one voice at the same time. I followed it, dodging cooped-up ten-year-olds left and right, until I came to the door of the boys' dorm room. I hesitated outside for a moment, my ear to the old wood.

It was definitely coming from inside.

I quickly opened the door and stepped in, my heart pounding. Inside were four boys sitting around on the beds. None of them had even the slightest hint of anything sinister about them and yet they all managed to look guilty. Mind you, since when did a group of unaccompanied small boys ever *not* look guilty? We all stared at each other for a full minute.

"What are you doing?" I asked.

"Nothing," they all said together. Nothing suspicious there at all, oh no.

I looked around. There wasn't anything else in the room that could have made those noises. It had to have come from the kids.

"Which of you was making that noise?" I asked. "That weird singing, whistling noise. I know it was coming from in here."

They looked at each other and then at the floor. One of them looked up at me, though. He shrugged.

"We all were," he said.

"Why?" I asked. "What is it?"

The boy that had spoken blinked and looked at the others. "We were only playing," he said. "It scares the girls. It's funny."

"Why?" I asked again. "Why does it scare the girls?"

The kids looked at each other again, and then the boy shrugged. "It's the sound the ghosts make," he said.

"The what?"

Another boy piped up. "The ghosts," he said. "The ones in the forest."

They all looked over to the window. I realized that they'd kept the curtains closed.

"Ghosts?" I said, doing my best to sound amused. "What makes you think there are ghosts in the forest?"

The first boy looked back over to me. "Because they make that sound," he said, with the kind of logic that makes sense only if you're ten.

"Right," I said. "Look. Do any of you know what it is? Really?"

They all stared at me like they didn't understand a word I'd said.

"Sure," I said eventually. "I get it. Ghosts, yeah? That's absolutely what it is. Look, just – try to keep the noise down, OK? Some of us are trying to think."

I left the room again, pulling the door shut behind me. I kept my fingers on the handle for a minute, feeling cold inside again and not sure why. The fact that the kids in there had heard the same thing I had was a good thing, wasn't it? At least it meant I wasn't downright crazy. OK, so I still didn't know what it was, but I was pretty sure I knew what it wasn't. I mean come on, what person in their right mind believes in ghosts?

I retreated to my room and finished unpacking my things. At lunchtime I fought my way through the insanity again and went down to the dining room. There was a buffet that Dorothea had put out for us, although that's probably too grand a term for it. It was basically sausages and mash served in big silver terrines that belonged in the same museum as the rest of the house.

I was spooning mash on to my plate when Mum came in. I glanced up at her and stopped. She seemed weirdly nervous. Nervous is not something I would usually associate with my mother. Tough, yes. Suits, yes. Take no prisoners, yes. Suffer no fools, yes. Nervous? Never in a million years. It would be like suggesting a velociraptor had suddenly developed a penchant for fluffy pink slippers. It made me think of her hands shaking after her confrontation with Dorothea over the ghost stories. I didn't like it.

Then Tomas came in, shutting the door behind him. He smiled at my mum.

"Thought I'd sneak away for five minutes," he confessed. "Hopefully being occupied with lunch will keep them quiet for that long, at least."

'Quiet' was evidently a relative term in Tomas's

111

dictionary, because I could definitely still hear the dull roar of child mania despite the fact that they were two rooms, a hallway and two shut doors away.

Mum didn't smile back at him, only frowned a bit. "I know they're bored with being stuck indoors," she said, "but I think it would be best if you kept them away from the attic level. It could be dangerous up there."

"Oh, sure," said Tomas, "you're absolutely right – it's kind of Dorothea's private space. That's why I tell the kids it's out of bounds. None of them go up there."

"They do, actually," Mum told him. "I saw a boy up there earlier. I heard footsteps as I was passing the stairs and there he was standing at the top. I called to him but he ran off."

Tomas frowned. "Really? Are you sure? Like I said, they all know it's out of bounds and they're good kids."

"Of course I'm sure. And I know they're good kids but I also know what I saw. So perhaps you should have another word with them. We don't want any accidents."

"You're right. I'll talk to him. Who was it? Did you see the boy come down again?"

"I didn't get close enough to see who it was. I followed him up the stairs, but he'd disappeared. He must have been hiding somewhere and then slipped back down here when I wasn't looking."

There was a brief pause, in which Tomas looked at my mother in a way I wasn't sure I liked. The door opened again and this time Dorothea scuttled in.

"Dorothea," Tomas said immediately. "Mrs Stromberg is worried that some of the children might have been up in the attic."

The housekeeper laughed. And when I say laughed, I mean that for about four seconds she emitted a sound like a chicken being strangled. "No."

"No?" asked Mum, her voice a little high. I guess she was still pretty pissed off about her last one-on-one encounter with Dorothea. "What do you mean 'No'?"

"The children know better than to go up there," said the old woman.

"Well, I saw a boy up there earlier today."

"No," said Dorothea, in a voice quiet with menace. "You did not. The children do not go up there. I would know if the children went up there."

"Perhaps this is the first time. Either way—"

"No," Dorothea said again, as if somehow the single word was enough to settle the matter.

Mum tried again. "Look, Dorothea, I—"

The housekeeper waved a hand. "Perhaps you are seeing things," she suggested, in a tone of voice that was as dismissive as the gesture. "It happens to some women."

I saw Mum's hackles rise. "*What?*"

Dorothea had already moved past her and was picking up some of the empty dishes. "Some women have weak minds," she said. "The snow makes them see things. It happens."

I don't think I'd ever seen Mum as angry as she was in that moment and with me for a kid, that's really saying something.

"How *dare* you?" she began. "I am telling you, I saw—"

Tomas stepped forwards, holding up his hands. "It's OK. I'll talk to the children. This will never happen again. All right?"

There was a silence, during which my mother and Dorothea didn't acknowledge either what Tomas had said or each other. Then the housekeeper headed for the door again. As she skittered past my mother,

I heard her speak, just loud enough for it to carry. It was a poisonous mutter, stealthy and vindictive.

"There was no child," she whispered.

I wanted my mum to *do* something. I don't know what – trip the old bat up, maybe? Send her sprawling on top of all her dumb, precious china? But Mum didn't do anything. I was watching her face and instead of angry, she looked ... scared. My fearless, take-no-prisoners mother looked afraid.

There was a horrible moment of silence.

"Well," Tomas said awkwardly. "I'd really appreciate it if you could spare some time to help me keep the kids occupied this afternoon. They're bored of me but they love you."

Mum looked up with a faint smile, though she didn't quite meet his eyes. "Of course. What did you have in mind?"

It wasn't until after they'd left that it occurred to me that Mum hadn't eaten any lunch.

Tomas and Mum tried to organize some games for the kids in their dining room, which didn't really lessen the noise but did at least keep them all in roughly the same place. I decided to get as far away from them as I could so I made for the library.

I figured nosing around it might be a little more interesting than watching paint dry. But when I opened the door, I found that Dad had beaten me to it. He was sitting at one of the tables with a map of the forest spread out in front of him. Beside it was his clipboard with the list of the felling equipment we'd found in the barn.

I didn't want to get roped into anything so I backed out again and closed the door behind me. I stood there for a minute, wondering what to do next. Then I remembered the office I'd found, the one with the desk full of someone else's junk.

Let's face it, I didn't have anything better to do, did I?

Still we dream.
Faces, places, mixed up and tattered.
They are not the forest. They are not the snow.
We circle, still lost.
Confused.

*Think of nothing but us,*
whisper the trees.
*You are ours. Remember us.*
*Remember what is owed.*
*Listen to the song.*

# Chapter Eleven

I stopped outside the door of the office and looked around to make sure no one saw me going in. Not that there was any reason why it should be a problem if they did – this was my home now, right? – but I was still wary of Dorothea. There was no one around, so I twisted the handle and stepped inside.

Everything was exactly as it had been when I saw it the first time. The study had two large windows in the external wall and there were shelves filled with more books lining the other three, except where the door and another big fireplace stood. There was an old, expensive-looking green leather armchair sitting in front of the fireplace. At the other end of the room, in front of the book-lined wall, was the large wooden desk. It was one of those that had leather set in the top – green again – with gold scrolling around the edge. The office chair was old and wooden. On the desk there was a green swivel lamp, an old-style telephone and those piles of papers. There was no computer, which besides being disappointing made the whole scene even more old-fashioned. The room made me feel as if I'd stepped back in time.

I sat down in the chair behind the desk, wondering who the last person was to sit in it before me and who the first person had been to sit in it, ever. I always find that kind of crazy to think about – how things were before you knew a place. There's so much about this life that you're never going to find out. And sure, most people would say that knowing who sat in the same chair as you doesn't matter in the slightest – that in the grand scheme of things, it's a stupid thing to think about. I guess that says a lot about me, right? I think about the fact that at some point in the future, someone will sit in this chair and they may not even know I existed. Like, my entire life at that second was that chair. It's what I was doing, right then, right there, and because of that it's everything I was in that moment. But to someone else it's as insignificant as dust. That's kind of chilling, in a way, isn't it? How little we matter, really, in the big stream of time. Things keep on going, regardless of whether we're there or not.

I opened the top right-hand drawer, just as I had the last time I'd looked through the desk, but this time I paid more attention. I lifted everything out and dumped it on top of the desk. Then I went through every piece of paper one by one. Now, some people get a kick out of reading other people's stuff but I think even the nosiest of them would have been bored to death with what I found in there. Everything was about the plantation – timber yields, quotas, labour costs, maintenance fees, yadda, yadda. Even the stuff about money didn't help make it interesting. I shoved everything back where it came from and went on to the next drawer, which was more of the same.

I was beginning to think about giving up. It was all just so much ... nothing. Then, in the middle drawer on the right side, I found something buried amid another ton of boring paperwork. It was a mid-sized notebook with a red leather cover, one of those that has a piece of black elastic that stretches from the back to the front to keep it closed. I picked it up and could tell straight away that it had something inside it. There was a bulge that made the front cover curve slightly.

I put it on the desk and opened it. In the front

of the notebook were seven photographs. Three were old black-and-white family pictures, like the one I'd found in the bedroom upstairs. It was the others that made me look twice, though. The four colour Polaroids.

I separated the Polaroids from the other photographs and looked at them one by one. As I did I felt a cold wind work its way in from outside and drift across my neck. Three of them were selfies of the same bloke. I'm not good with ages, but he could have been in his early thirties. He was pale with really blond hair, which made him look pretty much albino. I don't know if he actually was albino though, because I couldn't see his eyes. He was wearing big wraparound sunglasses in every one of the pictures.

It wasn't really him that creeped me out, even though his unsmiling face did have a touch of the Aryan grim reaper about it. It was what was going on in the background that was the real kicker. Each been taken in the wake of some nasty disaster that the guy had survived.

I could see snow in all of them so I guessed they'd all been taken in winter. In the first one I picked up, it looked as though the guy had shimmied up a tree to get a good angle, because it was quite high up and I could see the wisps of branches blurring the edge of the shot. There was a frozen lake and hanging over the edge of the lake was a jack-knifed truck. It had obviously slid off the road and on to the ice. The cab was right on the water's edge, the door hanging open where the driver had managed to escape. The ice had cracked under the weight of the truck and the split spread out in two mean, jagged pieces under the front wheel. The truck, which looked like one of the cage trailers we'd found in the barn, was leaning into the water, beginning to spill its load of logs off the back. That baby was going down, no question. I wondered how deep the lake was. The water under the sheared ice was pretty black.

In the second one, the guy was standing in front of a tree that had fallen right across a narrow road. That might not sound like much of a big deal, but this particular tree had smashed into the front of a red 4x4, which I'm guessing he'd been driving at the time. The windscreen was a web of cracks with a hole in it where the monster tree had whacked it on its way down. The dude was lucky the car industry's all about safety glass these days, because if that windscreen had shattered while he was behind the wheel, he'd have been left looking like something out of a horror film. Although he probably wouldn't have known that, because at the very least the glass would have slashed his eyes right out of his head.

The third showed a fire. With a weird lurch of my stomach I recognized the woodshed right near the house, the old one next to the equipment barn.

The final one was by far the creepiest though. It was the only one that didn't have the guy with sunglasses in the foreground. It was a blurred shot of some snow — no biggie, right? Except that on the snow were drops of blood, bright red against the white. Something about that particular picture really made my heart jump. The blood showed up too red, too bright, for it to be at night. Stuff like that should happen at night, right? And before you ask, no, I don't know what 'stuff' I mean.

I put all of the photographs down and stared at them for a bit, not quite sure what it was I'd found. Then I picked up the notebook they'd been in, in case there was an explanation, but although some pages seemed to have been torn out, there was nothing written in it at all. Then I picked up the photograph of the jack-knifed truck again and turned it over in case there was a date on it. Some people write them on photographs, right? Well, this person hadn't. Instead, on the back was written one word in a jagged scrawl. It said *Nails*. I picked up the one of the car. On the back it said *Sawn*. On the back of the one with the woodshed fire, in the same haphazard hand was written the word *Petrol*.

There was nothing written on the back of the one of the blood in the snow.

I stared at the photos for a while, trying to make sense of them, and as I did, I heard something. It drifted to me from somewhere indistinct, a small sound getting louder. It was footsteps, a little series of taps too regular to be anything else. I looked up at the door, because it seemed to me that they were coming closer, towards the room I was in. They grew closer and closer, until I was sure that whoever it was would walk right into the room but they didn't. The footsteps faded away again. The strange thing was that for a moment I thought they had gone behind me. But they couldn't have – there wasn't anything behind me except another bookcase. I turned to look, to make sure. Nothing.

Outside the room, the sound of the kids suddenly got louder. Tomas and Mum had obviously run out of containment strategies. I could hear them thumping about, shrieking and screaming, playing some sort of game that evidently involved running up and down the stairs while making as much noise as they possibly could. At that moment, I was back to not minding. Noise drives out the demons as well as daylight does. I went back to looking at the Polaroids.

You know what? To me those scrawled words on the back sounded like explanations for what was going on in the pictures. I mean nails under the tyres of a truck that big could probably cause it to jack-knife on icy ground, right? And *Petrol* written on the back of a photograph of a fire didn't strike me as being particularly cryptic, either. But still, what did that mean? I sure as hell didn't know.

The thumping outside got louder. There seemed to be some chanting going on – counting. I think the children were trying to see who could jump up and down the most stairs at once.

I pushed the Polaroids to one side and picked up the older photographs instead. They'd all been put together and I figured that had to mean something, even if I had no clue what. There didn't seem to be any relation between what was happening in the Polaroids and the family snaps from the Days of Yore. Then I realized something. When I'd first glanced at them, I'd assumed the photographs were all of the same family – the same one I'd found in the picture upstairs. I'd been fooled by the similar poses and the lack of colour. In reality they were all completely different groups of people. But they'd all obviously lived here, since every photograph had been taken right outside the main doors.

All three of the families had a stern-looking father and a distant-looking mother. One of the photographs showed just one little boy and the other two each had an older boy and a younger girl. Beside them there was the usual straggle of gaunt-looking servants. All of them were dressed up to the nines and staring at the camera without the single trace of a smile.

*BANG!*

The study door swung open so violently that it slammed against the bookcase behind it. I jumped and I dropped the photographs, scattering them on the floor. Dorothea stood in the doorway with a look of complete and utter fury on her face.

"You!" she shrieked, her voice almost drowned out by the tidal wave of the kids' wild, screaming laughter. "In the master's private room! How DARE you?"

My mouth dropped open but whatever noise I was planning to make was swallowed by a huge, resounding crack. It exploded from the hallway like a bomb going off.

Then the real screaming started.

# Chapter Twelve

I jumped up from the desk and went to the door, pushing past Dorothea and running down the hall. The first thing I saw was the massive, ragged hole in the floor. It was right below the first step of the main staircase. The children were gathered around it, some on their knees, yelling into it. Others were standing back looking terrified and tearful.

My mother appeared, Tomas close behind her. Dad ran up behind me.

"What's happened?" Tomas bellowed. "Marcus – tell me!"

The boy he'd collared for an explanation was pale but not crying. "It's Alisa," he pointed. "She fell…"

My mum put her hands up to her mouth. "Oh my God!"

"Alisa?" Tomas shouted into the hole. "Can you hear me?"

There was no answer. Mum got on her knees

beside the hole in the floor, leaning forwards. "I can't see her!"

I pushed through the sobbing kids, all standing around like useless statues. "Get out of the way," I told them. "If the floor's rotten, standing here is stupid. Go upstairs, go outside – go anywhere. But not here."

My dad nodded. "That's right. Kids, I know you're scared but we have to deal with this. Go on, out of the way, please. We'll look after Alisa."

"Is it a cellar?" Mum was asking, still on her knees.

Tomas looked grim. "It must be but I didn't know it was there. I didn't know the house even had a basement level. We have to get down there."

"Dorothea!" my father shouted. "Where is she? Can't she hear what's going on? Dorothea!"

I turned to look down the corridor – she'd been standing right there in the doorway of the study but now she'd vanished. I assumed she'd gone into the room but then I saw her appear out of the door that led to the kitchen. I didn't have time to wonder how she'd got there.

"There's been an accident," my mum said breathlessly. "One of the girls has fallen. We have to get into the cellar."

"Show us where the door is," Tomas said.

The old woman stared at the hole but didn't seem particularly interested in it or the poor kid lying somewhere down there in the dark. "What a mess," she said, with a trace of disgust. "Running about. Making noise. Only herself to blame."

My dad went for her. For a second I really thought he was going to throttle the old bint but he settled for grabbing her arm. "Show us where the door is," he yelled, right in her face.

Dorothea pulled her arm away and looked at him with hate. "Boarded up," she said shortly, like that was any sort of explanation.

Tomas jumped to his feet. My mum was still yelling into the hole as though if she shouted loudly enough the kid would answer. Instead of, you know, being dead and therefore unable to use her vocal cords, which I thought was probably more likely.

"For God's sake!" Tomas yelled. *Where. Is. It?*"

Dorothea eyed Tomas and Dad and then shuffled away. We followed – all except Mum, who was still trying to get Alisa to answer. The housekeeper took us down the corridor that led to the right from the entrance hall.

"Hurry up!" hissed my dad, clearly having to restrain himself from shoving the old woman into a run.

Dorothea ignored him. She stopped in front of a large wooden dresser that stood against the wall opposite the dining room. I'd seen it before but not really taken notice of it. It was full of old plates and cups – the sort of stuff your grandparents never use but have stacked up in cupboards. The housekeeper jerked her chin at it.

"Behind there?" asked Tomas. "Christ. All right." He and my dad took up position on either side of it. They started yanking it away from the wall with violent jerks that sent bits of the crockery crashing noisily to the floor.

"No!" Dorothea shouted. She tried to wrestle with Tomas but he shook her off. More and more plates and bowls smashed against the wooden floor under our feet, until the corridor was a sea of patterned porcelain shards.

Behind the dresser was a rough wooden door. It had been nailed shut with planks criss-crossed over it.

My dad rubbed a shaking hand over his face. "I don't believe this!"

Tomas didn't even pause. He yanked the arms of his sweater down over his fingers, then hooked them behind the top plank and began to heave. Dad joined in and then I did, too. The wood was rough, with nails sticking out of it all over the place as if it had been blocked up in a hurry. The first plank came away in a shower of splinters that hit me in the face. The second was easier as the wood seemed to be rotten.

Over my shoulder I could still hear Mum. She'd given up shouting down to the girl for an answer now. Her voice was much more soothing. It reminded me of when I was sick as a little kid. She'd sit there for hours beside my bed, stroking my hair and talking to me. For a second I wondered when it was that she'd stopped doing that.

The last plank came away but we still had to get the door open. Would you believe it was locked? None of us said anything – I don't think anything would have surprised us by this point. Tomas tried the door and then raised one leg and smashed his foot against the lock.

Inside, the dark was thick and soupy. Even with the light coming down through the hole in the floor, it was almost impossible to see anything.

I pulled my phone out of my pocket and thumbed it on. It wasn't much but it was better than nothing.

Beyond the door was a flight of stairs. The pool of light from the phone was barely enough to see a couple of steps ahead. Tomas edged forwards – I think he was worried that wood might be rotten too. Dad held me back until Tomas had got safely to the bottom. Then he went next, with me following.

The faint light from the hole above filtered down into a rough circle. I could see a shape on the floor – the kid. There was a noise, too, something other than Mum's mutterings from above. It was a groaning, moaning sound. It was coming from the body.

"Alisa?" Tomas called quietly.

She didn't look in a good way – not dead, which was a relief, obviously, but not completely conscious, either. Once we'd seen what else was wrong with her, I think we all decided that was a good thing.

"Oh God," my dad muttered.

There was a lot of blood. The kid – Alisa – had broken her leg in the fall. And when I say broken, I mean that the bone had snapped in two and one splintered end had ripped right through the skin. Seriously, I've never seen anything like that in real life before. Smashed bone and gristle glistened in the light from my phone. Her blood was like a dark lake spreading out from where she lay, picking up little flecks of dust from the dirty floor that floated like miniature flotsam on the surface as it grew.

"We – we can't move her," my dad said, his voice pretty shaky. "That's the injury we can see – what about the ones we can't?"

He had a point. Also, I could already imagine how much moving her was going to hurt.

Tomas shouted up through the hole. "Call the air ambulance!"

There was the faint sound of shuffling and then running feet tapped across the wood over our heads. While we waited for Mum to come back, Tomas pulled his sweater off and covered Alisa with it as he tried to check her over. He talked to her the whole time, small words that I don't think meant anything at all. They were just sounds.

The tapping came back.

"They can't come," my mother's voice said,

sounding slightly desperate as it floated down through the darkness. "The snow – this freak weather front – it's turned into a severe blizzard. They can't fly until it clears!"

"But – what do we do?" my father asked, with an edge of panic.

"We've got to get her out of here," Tomas said, his voice hoarse. "We need a stretcher."

"But—"

"There's no choice," Tomas cut him off. "We can't leave her here. If there's no one else, we have to move her. We have to get her to the nearest hospital. OK?"

It was obvious that we weren't going to find a stretcher. Tomas smashed the cellar door off its hinges and we used that instead.

Alisa came around as we started to move her. I've never heard the sound of pure pain before. Her screams were so loud that they lit up the dark in that cellar better than a flashlight would. She passed out again as they lifted her and laid her on the door but I carried on hearing that noise for ages afterwards.

They put her into the back of our 4x4. They'd

covered the kid in blankets but her face was as white as death. I really couldn't see how she was going to survive the drive.

"I can't leave the other children," Tomas said, his face grey. "They're going to need me…"

"It's all right," Mum told him, squeezing his arm. "I'll go with her. We'll look after her, Tomas. I promise." She climbed into the back of the car, wedging her back against the glass and her shins against the felled door on which Alisa lay.

Dad pulled out as if he was a rally driver but I guess if I'd been driving, I would have done the same thing. The hospital was miles away and they were driving on snow.

Tomas and I stood there, watching the car disappear down the track. The snow had started to fall again – harder, faster – and there was a cold wind picking up.

"I'd better see if I can calm the others down," Tomas muttered, before trudging back inside the house.

I followed a few minutes later. I could hear Tomas's voice, low and soothing, talking to the group. There was the sound of crying, too, sniffles and sobs. I looked at the hole, huge and dark. I was glad there hadn't been more light down there. I was glad that none of the kids had been able to see what a state Alisa was in. At least the shape of their nightmares wouldn't be specific.

The song calls us.
It weaves around the trees.
We follow it.

*Hurry,* say the trees.
*There is a debt that must be paid.*
*It is already late.*
*Hurry.*

# Chapter Thirteen

I went back to the cellar. I'm not sure why. Maybe it was those nails, hammered so hurriedly into the planks to seal it shut. That most definitely had to mean something. It might sound weird that I wasn't more creeped out by the prospect of going down into that cellar again alone, especially given my sudden existential fear of trees but I honestly wasn't. I might have been in shock. I guess curiosity really does kill the cat.

I got to the bottom of the stairs and waved my phone around but there wasn't much to see. It was mostly empty. I got a slight frisson of excitement when the phone picked out a shape lurking behind one of the pillars holding the floor above up but it turned out to be a broken chair. There were a few other bits and pieces – knackered bits of furniture and what may or may not have been plantation equipment. They were all either broken or rusted and therefore useless. Exactly the kind of stuff you find in abandoned cellars. Nothing to see here, folks, move along, please.

In fact, I was thinking that I might as well do exactly that when I noticed something on the wall in the far corner. It was beyond the hole that Alisa had made on her way down. I picked my way around the edge of the pool of blood on the floor to take a closer look.

It was a series of planks that had been nailed over what must have once been a door. Whoever had done it had been in a hurry so I figured it was probably the same person who had boarded up the door at the top of the cellar stairs. They were criss-crossed and uneven. Some had split where they had been hammered just a bit too hard. One had a chink in it, a little sliver of wood that had disintegrated under the nail. I pressed my face closer to see what was behind it but there was just more wood – probably the door that had been covered up. I stepped back and tried to work out where a door here could possibly lead. Another room? But why board that up when the main door to the basement level had already been sealed shut?

Why board up a cellar door at all, except to stop something getting out? But there wasn't anything down here. Nothing at all except a few bits of old, broken junk. To stop something getting in, maybe? But where from? The door that had been boarded up couldn't lead outside. From what I could work out it was pretty much under the start of the hallway that led to the library and study.

Something moved beside me. I swore harder than I ever have in my life. The 'something' was Dorothea. A second before the battery in my phone died, I saw her face. You know that trick you play on people at Halloween, when you hold a torch below your chin and make a scary face? Well, she didn't need to make a scary face.

Her voice came out of the soupy darkness like gas. "Easy to get stuck down here," she whispered.

I was shaking like a leaf. I scrabbled around for my phone like a loser, grabbing it up before making for the faint light filtering down the stairs. I didn't hear Dorothea come back up behind me but the blood was pounding so hard in my ears by that point that I was pretty much deaf to everything besides my own heartbeat.

I ran all the way up to my room and slammed the door shut behind me. I stood there for a while, staring at my blue crate but not really seeing it. I tried to calm myself down. *Nothing happened,* I kept telling myself. *You're OK. You're fine.* After a while I stopped thinking that my heart was pumping so hard that my chest was about to split in two.

My curtains were still open. I wandered slowly to the window and looked out.

The outdoor lights had come on. They cast yellow light out into the twilight, reaching as far as the edge of the trees. For a moment, I thought I saw the boy again. The one from the forest, the one I'd assumed had been playing hide and seek in front of that dying tree. He was standing under my window, staring up at me.

I dragged up the window to get a closer look but by then he'd moved and I couldn't see him. By now the adrenaline faded. I'd passed beyond scared and into the realms of being really pissed off. It had been a real pig of a day. Hell, it was turning into a pig of a life. So if that kid out there thought he could mess with me, he had another thing coming.

I went back downstairs. I could hear faint noise

coming from the dining room where the rest of the kids were gathered. Some of them were crying and I could hear the murmur of Tomas's voice, still trying to soothe them.

I kept my eyes fixed on the front door the whole time as I made my way down the stairs but it didn't open. I still had my boots on – I rarely take them off wherever I am, another of my habits that drives Mum completely insane. I made it round the hole in the floor, headed straight for the door and went out into the snow.

Night had fallen as if someone had flicked a switch. It swarmed, thick and black beyond the pale glow of the lights fixed on the walls. I swear it hadn't been that dark when I'd looked out of my window a few minutes earlier. The wind had got stronger, too, whirling the snow faster and faster. The blizzard had come for us.

I pushed on, even as the storm got worse. I stayed in the light near the wall of the house, looking for footprints – I figured I'd be able to tell where the kid had come from as well as where he'd gone– but there were none. They couldn't have disappeared this quickly, not even with the falling snow that was getting steadily worse with each passing minute, but I couldn't find them anywhere. I rounded the corner of the house and glanced up at my window.

I turned in a circle searching for those prints, but there was no sign of them. It must have taken me less than three minutes to get out there. I looked up at my window again, wondering if I'd misjudged where the kid had been standing. Maybe he'd been further away from the house than I thought?

I walked right up to the edge of the light and ended up so close to the forest that I nearly took my eye out on one of the dead lower branches. My attention was fixed on the ground, searching for those damned footprints. Nothing. No indication that any kid but me had walked on this snow. It was as though he'd never been there. And still the blizzard got worse. I could hardly see by then, frozen flakes stabbing my forehead and cheeks like icy bee stings.

Another gust of wind stirred the trees and this one set them whispering. I could hear it even over the sound of the storm. The noise crept down my spine. I looked up. The night hung in clumps around the trunks; deeper, darker shadows spreading by the second. I thought I saw movement and squinted –

I wasn't going to go any further. No way. But there was something moving under there, I was sure of it. I thought about the boy I'd seen in the forest – he hadn't even been slightly freaked out, sitting there staring at that dying tree. Was this the same kid? Had he gone right into the forest to avoid me seeing him? But if he had, where were the footprints? And why would he do that anyway?

Whatever the something was moved again but it wasn't a person, not even a small one. I could hardly see it through the whipping snow but I swear it slid out of one shadow and into another, low to the ground, fluid as water. I heard a sound. It began like the whispering of the trees but lifted clear of them, louder. A whine that was almost a howl.

I went back to the house, holding my arms up over my face to keep the snow out of my eyes. By the time I'd shut the front doors behind me I had decided I must have been wrong. There couldn't have been a boy out there, could there?

I'd been seeing things. That was all. That explanation didn't seem as scary.

Not at the time, anyway.

# Chapter Fourteen

There weren't any more games that night. My dad called to say that they had reached the hospital and wouldn't be back until sometime the next day at the earliest. At dinner the kids ate in silence. Then they went to bed. Then so did Tomas. Then so did I. The house already seemed empty, somehow.

Twice I woke in the dark to the tune of the kids' nightmares. I thought about getting up and going to the screamers but as I was thinking about it, I heard Tomas's voice. I could see how the tree-hugger might be soothing, under the circumstances. More soothing than I would be, anyway.

In the night the blizzard died away again. The snow was still on hiatus when I got up the next morning. More surprising still was that at some time during the night, the coach had limped its way up the track and was now standing outside. I found out later that the driver had taken advantage of the gap in the weather. He'd arrived at about 4 a.m. but instead of waking everyone up had slept in his seat. Some people are just too dedicated to their jobs. There must be twenty spare beds in this house. Not to mention the fact that it's warm.

The kids all looked as if their pets had been brutally murdered. The quiet was beginning to get to me. Tomas loaded them all on to the coach after breakfast. I hung around, watching from beside the front door as he counted them in.

Once they were all aboard, he came to say goodbye to me. Dorothea was off skulking somewhere and I guess in his mind I was standing in for my parents. I should have left well alone but for some reason I'd been thinking about that kid again – the one I thought I'd seen in the snow under my window.

"Last night," I said, "one of the kids was outside. A boy. He was standing under the trees, staring up at the house."

Tomas didn't say anything, just gave me a strange look.

I shrugged. "I thought, you know – shock, or something? Maybe they should … talk to someone?"

"What time was this?" he asked.

"Er – don't know. Just after the … after Mum and Dad left with Alisa. I looked out of the window and he was just standing there in the snow."

Tomas shook his head. "They were all in the dining room until dinner. I kept everyone together, trying to calm them down. There wasn't anyone missing."

I frowned. "I'm not lying."

"I'm not saying you are, I…" Tomas sighed. He looked pretty tired. "Look. Get on the coach, now. Tell me if you can see the kid you mean, OK?"

I should have said no. I should have just taken him at his word, let them trundle off into the snow and thought no more about it. Instead I did as he said and clambered on to the bus.

Rows and rows of faces looked back at me. They were all pale, all miserable. Even the ones on the back seat were sitting still and quiet. I looked at each one but couldn't see the boy I was looking for. Tomas climbed up on to the bus beside me.

"Well?" he asked.

"Yeah," I muttered. Then I pointed at a random kid three rows back, by the window. "It was him."

Tomas narrowed his eyes at me. I knew he knew

I was lying but all he said was, "OK. Thanks. I'll be sure to talk to him."

I nodded, stuck my hands in my pockets and got off the bus.

"Oh yeah," I said, before the door closed. "I meant to check something else with you. The previous owner."

"Yes?" Tomas asked, impatient. "What about him?"

"What's his name again?"

"Erik. Erik Gran."

"He has dark hair, right? Dark hair and dark eyes?"

Tomas shook his head. "No. Erik is your stereotypical Swede. Very fair hair, fair skin, blue eyes." Then he fixed me with another strange expression. "Look," he said. "I know that your dad doesn't take me seriously … but he should. You should leave this place. All of you, as soon as you can. Before it's too late."

I didn't know what to say to that. I probably should have asked something like, "Too late for what?" but I didn't. I watched as the doors closed and the coach pulled away. When I turned back to the house, I found Dorothea standing on the doorstep. Her face was as pleasant as a freshly landed salmon. She stared at me for a second and then disappeared through the doors. For the first time, it occurred to me that Cruella De Vil and I were now the only ones there. Two people, in that huge, empty house and she was the one with access to the knives. Comforting.

My parents arrived back mid-afternoon. From my bedroom I heard the purr of the engine as the 4x4 drove up to the house – that's how quiet the place was now. I went downstairs as the door opened. When I got to the bottom of the stairs, I found Mum standing in the doorway. She was as still as a marble statue and almost as white, staring at the gaping hole in the floor. Her eyes looked huge, with circles around them as dark as bruises. The look on her face scared me. Her eyes looked hollow, like maybe there wasn't anything behind them.

"Mum? Is everything OK?" I asked. "Is Alisa…"

Mum didn't seem to hear me. She carried on staring at that dark, ragged hole.

"She's going to be all right," Dad said, answering for Mum as he appeared in the doorway behind her. He looked exhausted.

"He means she's not going to die," Mum said, her voice coming from somewhere very far away and very empty. "Whether she'll be able to walk properly again, to run and jump, and…"

Dad put his arm round her shoulders and pulled her closer. "Alisa will be OK," he told her.

"It was my fault," she said shakily. "I should have been paying more attention. I should have known what they were doing and stopped them. I should have—"

"Stop it," Dad said. "It's not your fault. Of course it isn't!"

I stood there on the stairs, feeling awkward. Behind them, the door was still open, cold air gusting in. In the few moments since they had returned it had started snowing again.

Mum pulled away from Dad and nodded jerkily at the hole. "We should cover that up," she said.

The wind gusts.
The forest roars.
The snow thickens.

We let the song lead us.

*Yes*, say the trees.
*You are not lost.*
*You are ours.*
*You are us.*
*And we will not forgive.*

# Chapter Fifteen

Dad was convinced that the snow was going to stop.

"It's too early for this to be the start of winter proper, even this far north," he kept saying. "This will blow over again, you'll see. Then we'll have time to get properly battened down for when the real snow starts in a month or so."

He said this like he had any idea of what was normal up here. As if he'd never even heard of the term 'climate change' and that we might have put ourselves right in the middle of the nitty-gritty sharp end of it. I knew what he was doing, though. It was obvious. He was trying to convince himself that he was right because saying something enough times out loud somehow turns it into the truth.

I think he was scared, too, although not about the weather.

Mum wasn't doing well. What had happened to Alisa had triggered something in her, some depression that was quickly swallowing her up. Since they'd got back, she'd moped around, staring out of the windows. Dad kept trying to encourage her into doing things, like going out for a walk with him in the snow or reading a book from the library, but she didn't seem to want to do anything at all. Even if she started something, she'd only stick at it for a few minutes. After that she'd wind up staring into space again. I had never known her like that before – I was used to her being the spinning motor at the centre of our family that kept everything going no matter what.

Dad and I didn't even mention what was happening to her. It was like we were hoping that whatever had settled on her would float away again pretty soon. I didn't try to talk to her, either, not at first. I didn't know how, I guess. She was usually the one telling Dad and me what we should be doing. Now she wasn't even there, and we didn't know what to do and had no one to explain it to us, because the person who would usually do that was away. She spent more and more time in their room but I didn't go to see her, not even when Dad had to take her food because she started not coming down for meals. I didn't ask Dad about her, either. It wasn't that I didn't want to know how she was doing or that I didn't think about her. I just … didn't know how, that's all. What was I supposed to say? "Hey, Dad – how's Mum doing today? Still staring at the wall?"

The busted floor was one of the things that Mum seemed most disturbed by. Both of us had found her standing beside the hole where Alisa had fallen, staring into the dark cellar underneath. I know that freaked Dad out as much as it did me. So we boarded up the broken floor, or at least we tried to. There was a bit right in the middle that we couldn't do anything about. So we dragged a bright blue tarp over it and left it at that.

Anyway, the snow didn't stop for a full week after Tomas and the kids had left. Blizzard after blizzard blew up around the house out of a sky that was now permanently grey and heavy. Outside the trees were constantly moving, whipping their branches back and forth, their whole trunks leaning this way and that in the wind. The days grew shorter, the light fading into a permanent blue-black gloom that made us all squint. I could see Dad getting more and more antsy, but he continued to spout his 'it's too early' mantra, even while the main road into Storaskogen grew clogged with drifted snow. He worried about electricity and dug out a generator in case the power gave out. He also started stockpiling candles. I worried about food supplies but that didn't seem to be a problem. Dorothea continued to trundle out of the kitchen every day with a medley of uninteresting meals and she didn't seem to be worried in the slightest. In fact, her eyes had taken on a satisfied gleam, as if she'd called in this weather front herself to spite us.

She spoke to me, once. It was just a whisper as I passed her on the stairs. "Should have gone," she said. "Should have gone with all the others. Too late now."

I tried to pretend she'd said nothing at all. But I couldn't forget the 'too late' bit, however much I tried. That was what Tomas had said as well. Too late for what?

Every night I went to bed and looked out at the trees. They looked like lines and lines of angry people. Their branches were a million fists, all shaking at the house. None of them ever fell in the wind. How was that even possible, when we kept finding smashed tiles on the gravel outside where the wind had ripped them off the roof?

Then, two weeks to the day after Tomas and the kids had escaped, Dad came down to breakfast on his own. He had big dark circles under his eyes.

"Where's Mum?" I asked, like I didn't know.

Dad's eyes flickered to mine for a moment. "She'll be down in a bit. She's just taking a bit longer to get up this morning."

"OK…" I wanted to believe him as much as he wanted to believe himself but we both knew it was more likely that this was a yet another day where she wouldn't leave her room at all. Back in Stockholm, she'd gone to the gym every morning before work. But then, we weren't in Stockholm, were we? We were stuck in the butt-end of nowhere, in the snow. The snow that wasn't going to stop falling, no matter how much we were hoping it would.

"I don't think this snow is going to stop," Dad said suddenly, as if he'd somehow read my mind.

I swallowed the bite of roll I'd been chewing on but I didn't really know what to say even once my mouth was empty. It hadn't really been a question, had it?

And besides, he was the only one there who hadn't realized this gold nugget of truth weeks before.

"We need to prepare ourselves for the winter as quickly as possible," Dad went on. "That means we need a lot more wood for the fires. I thought we'd have more time to bring in stock from the drying shed but apparently not. So we'll have to do it now."

I nodded, swallowing another bite of breakfast. "Where's the drying shed?"

"Out on the boundary of the new plantation," he said, "not far from where Tomas took us that time. He pointed out the route to me as we walked."

I felt this big pit open up in my chest. "We need to bring in logs from out there? That's … that's a long way. Can't we take them from that other woodshed? The one next to the barn? There's loads in there, isn't there?"

Dad shook his head. "That's not enough to last us right through winter. We need to fill the other shed, too."

"How are we supposed to do that? There's only two of us!"

"We'll have to take one of the new trucks. The one with the hydraulic arm."

I stared at him. "Do you know how to drive it?"

He didn't meet my eye. "Not exactly. I was going to get a local to come and train me before I had to use it myself but that's out of the question now. I'll manage."

I thought about that Polaroid I'd found, the vicious comma of the jack-knifed truck hanging over the dark, watery oblivion of that frozen lake.

"OK…" I said. I put down my half-eaten roll. Suddenly I didn't feel that hungry any more.

"Wrap up, all right?" he said, standing up. "I'll meet you out at the main doors in twenty minutes. We need to get a move on. Today's going to be a long day."

I watched him leave, my mouth dry. I wasn't sure what I was more worried about – Dad trying to drive a piece of heavy machinery that could mince a human skull in one swipe, or going out there into the forest again. If the drying shed was on the boundary of the new plantation, that meant we'd be close to the old forest. Ever since that first trip out there I'd been trying hard to forget what I'd seen when I stumbled on the trees Erik had butchered. There was no way I wanted to see it again.

The door from the kitchen opened. It didn't make a sound, just swung outwards on silent hinges to slice a narrow black rectangle into the dreary wallpaper. Dorothea stepped out of it and stood just inside the room like an oversized gargoyle. She looked at me with a twisted little smile on her face but she didn't say anything. I didn't say anything either.

I left my unfinished breakfast where it was and went upstairs to dig out two extra sweaters and my all-weather jacket and trousers. Dad was already waiting when I got back down again but there was still no sign of Mum. Outside I could hear another blizzard starting up, the wind howling at the four walls, daring us to step outside.

"Ready?" Dad asked, once we'd pulled on our outer layers. "Let's go."

I really didn't see how we were going to be able to find our way anywhere in that weather. We could barely see down the steps outside the front door, for a start. I followed the bulk of Dad's outline around the side of the house, eyes squinted against the billowing snow. As soon as we stepped out of the lee of the wall, the wind sliced across my face like a cleaver. I had to turn my head to breathe at all. I ended up facing the wall of trees that signified the dark mass of the forest's edge. The firs were writhing in the wind, their spindly branches thrashing about, angry and violent.

I turned again to keep myself moving forwards. I held my breath and pushed into the wind, its razor-sharp edge hacking at my face. By the time we reached the middle barn and battled our way through the door, Dad and I were both breathless. We hadn't even gone a hundred paces.

"OK," Dad managed. He started to walk towards the wall of vehicles in front of us as he said, "It's the six-wheeler we need, so…"

He stopped talking mid-sentence. At first I couldn't see why. Then I stepped up beside him.

The wide tractor tyres of the machine we'd been intending to take out had been slashed. I don't mean that someone had stuck a knife through the thick hide of the wheels here and there – they'd been *eviscerated*. The rubber hung down in long, fleshy black streamers that didn't seem like they belonged to a vehicle at all. It wasn't just one of the tyres, either. It was all of them. And it wasn't just the six-wheeler – it was every piece of wheeled equipment we had. They were all completely ruined.

I stared at the mess. I couldn't begin to understand how someone might have managed it. The tyres were shredded, the strips all a uniform width, as if Wolverine had come along and merrily taken swipe after swipe at our machinery with his claws.

"Tomas," Dad said, in a strangled voice.

I looked at him. "What?"

"Tomas did this. Before he left."

There was a buzzing in my ears. I frowned, trying to work it out. "I don't think—"

"He wanted to stop me clearing his precious old forest. Didn't he?" Dad wasn't actually asking me. I don't think he was really talking to me at all. He was staring at the devastation in front of us, breathing hard, his face white. "He wanted to sabotage us. He did this."

"But he didn't leave the house," I said. "That night before they left he was with the kids the whole time—"

"Then he did it before."

"But…"

Dad spun towards me. I don't think I've ever seen him as angry as he was then. His fury hit me as though I'd walked straight into a wall. I took a step back.

"Who else?" Dad demanded. "Eh? Who else would have been strong enough to do this?"

The instant answer that had popped into my head – Dorothea – died. Because Dad was right, wasn't he? That rubber was eight centimetres thick at the treads. Even with a knife, cutting these tyres to shreds would have taken considerable muscle. Muscle that Dorothea didn't have. And who else could it have been?

*What* else could it have been?

Dad turned on his heel and marched back towards the door.

"Where are you going?" I asked, still reeling from our discovery and the idea that Tomas hated us enough to do something like this when he knew we were going to be stuck here.

"To call the police," Dad muttered, already outside.

It wasn't until I'd followed him outside that I realized the blizzard had stopped. There was no wind at all – the air was calm and what snow was left in the air was floating gently to the ground. The

164

trees had stopped moving. They were still; as still as I'd ever seen them.

*They know what's happened,* I thought. And then I wished I hadn't, because that was downright crazy.

# Chapter Sixteen

Back in the house, I sat on the stairs with my elbows on my knees, listening to Dad argue with the police officer on the other end of the line.

"That's ridiculous," he said. "What good is that to me? Why can't you go and arrest him now?" There was a pause and then Dad said, "I know it was him! And the evidence is here, so why not—?" He broke off, then muttered something else more quietly and put the phone down.

He turned round, his shoulders bowed as he looked over at me. "They say they can't get here until the snow clears. This weather front came in so quickly and the main road to Storaskogen is completely cut off. They'll send a helicopter, but only to evacuate us, not to investigate a 'petty' crime like this. And they won't issue an arrest warrant without evidence. Which they won't be able to gather until they can send an investigative team."

I tangled my fingers together but then the action made me think of the branches of the firs twisting around each other and I pulled them apart again. "So ... they're going to come and evacuate us, right?"

"No."

"No? Dad—"

"This is our home," he said roughly. "We are not going to be forced out of it. If we leave now, that criminal has won. And I won't let him win. Understand?"

"Then what are we going to do?"

"We need more wood," Dad said. "We'll have to find another way."

"What other way is there?"

He made a face. He clearly already knew how his next suggestion was going to go down. "I've been reading some of the books in the library, about how they used to log out here. You know, back in the old days."

I already didn't like the way this was going. "And...?"

"Before they had motorized equipment, they shifted felled logs with horses. In harnesses."

"We don't have any horses," I pointed out.

He nodded. "I know. We'll have to rig up harnesses for ourselves. Mum will have to help, too. With the three of us hauling a tree at a time, we'll manage it."

I stared at him. "You have got to be kidding."

Dad spread his hands, palms up. "We have to get more wood. Do you understand? How cold do you think this place is going to get if we run out of fuel? Very cold, is the answer. Too cold."

I shook my head and stood up. "This is insane. This whole thing is insane. *You're insane.*" I could hear my voice getting louder and higher with every syllable but I couldn't stop it. "Bringing us here in the first place! Thinking we were the kind of people who could live this life! Did you *want* to kill us? Was that your plan? Is that why you brought us here?"

Dad took a step towards me, the fury I'd seen on his face earlier back again with a vengeance. When he spoke, it was in a yell. "Enough! It wasn't—" He stopped short, swallowing whatever it was he'd been about to say. He clenched his fists, trying to get a hold of his anger. "We don't have time for this. There is no other way. All right? I'm going to get your mother. Get the snow shoes out, we'll need them."

He pushed past me and went upstairs.

The snow stayed away as all three of us left the house. We trudged over the calf-deep snow to nothing more than a light breeze. It was the longest period without a blizzard in days. I kept my eyes on my feet, concentrating on dragging the heavy length of rope Dad had handed to me as we'd left. Even though I was trying not to look at the trees on either side of us, I could tell they were laughing. It must have looked hilarious to them, three humans dwarfed by their magnitude, heading out to drag one of them back to the house with us. We had all these machines that were supposed to help us cut them down and we couldn't use any of them. All we had were our frail little bodies.

If I'd been a tree, I probably would have seen the funny side, too. Humans always think they're at the top of the food chain. But take away all their gadgets and it doesn't take much to change that. A really bad dump of snow, for example, or being out in the middle of nowhere alone. Or mostly alone.

Dad walked in front of me with Mum. She

hadn't said much since we'd left the house, but she'd smiled at me – really smiled at me – when she came downstairs, so I guess that was something. She seemed quite happy to be outside.

We followed the narrow path that Tomas had taken us out on during that first expedition. Maybe I was getting used to the lay of the land, or perhaps it was because it was covered in snow instead of pine needles, but I could tell it was a path more clearly this time. It formed a snowy canal between the trees, the width of one planting line and dead straight. All around us, everything was silent apart from the occasional *whhhump-whhhump-whhhump* of snow sliding from branches.

We reached a clear fork in the path where to the left the track widened to the width of two planting lines.

"It's this way," Dad said, turning to us. "I've looked at the plans and it shouldn't be more than a quarter of a mile along this track, OK? We're nearly there."

I nodded but didn't say anything. He started off again, heading along the new track. I glanced back the way we had come. The rope I carried had dragged its tail in the snow behind me, cutting a deep groove in the snow. It had sliced through all the prints our snowshoes had left so that they blurred into nothing. They didn't look like marks left by humans at all – it was as if we hadn't even passed this way.

*People go missing in this forest all the time.*

The words filled my head even though I tried to push them away. I hitched the rope up over my shoulder, then turned and headed after Mum and Dad. I still didn't look at the trees but I could feel them there, looming darkly over me. Right then, there was no sound at all except for my breathing.

Then a different sort of bulk appeared in front of us – the drying barn. It was larger than any of the other buildings we had on the plantation except for the house itself, with its front open to the forest. Inside were stacks and stacks of felled trees, de-branched but otherwise uncut. All of them were huge. Dad and I stood next to each other, catching our breath and looking up at them. I wondered how many of them had come from that bit of the old-growth forest that Erik had started to log.

"You really think we're going to be able to haul these all the way back to the house?" I asked.

Dad paused. "Yes," he said, in the type of voice he uses when he thinks a decisive tone will make up for the fact that he knows he's saying something that's blatantly wrong.

But, like he'd said earlier, what choice did we have?

"Let's … find a smallish one, yeah?" I suggested.

He at least had the grace to nod at that.

We'd been looking for a few minutes when the sound drifted to me through the trees. I hadn't heard that high, whooping wail of a song for a while. I'd almost forgotten it but there it was, as weird as the first time I'd heard it. Whatever was making it was close by and getting closer by the second. I couldn't help but listen to it. It was hypnotic. It got inside my head. I tried to focus, tried to work out if it really was coming closer or whether it just sounded that way because I was listening to it so carefully.

I still couldn't work out what it was. It couldn't be a voice. It was too high, too looping, for that. It sounded hollow, I decided, like the wind whistling through a dead tree. *Or,* insisted a part of my mind I tried not to take any notice of, *through a hunting horn*. Because what was there to hunt around here but us? And I didn't want *that* thought taking up any space in my head at all.

Then something occurred to me. I looked around and a cold that had nothing to do with the snow began to work its way down my neck. Dad was clambering on one of the piles. Apart from me, Dad and the pile of wood, the shed was empty.

"Dad?" I said. "Where's Mum?"

He stopped and looked around with a frown.

"Ingrid?" he called.

There was no answer.

"Mum?" I tried, walking to the other side of the woodpile as Dad jumped to the ground.

There was no sign of her.

"Ingrid!" Dad shouted from the front of the barn, her name shivering out into the air and catching against the branches beyond.

"Mum!" I yelled, trying to penetrate that darkness beneath the lowest branches, trying to send my call into the tunnels between the lines of trees.

There was sheer silence. The song had stopped. Even the firs were quiet. Waiting for something.

Watching us.

Then it started to snow again. There was no wind, no blizzard, just huge soft flakes drifting out of the sky.

"Find her trail," Dad said, his voice on the verge of panic. "Quickly, before its covered by the snow!"

We separated, eyes searching the old snow as new snow silently joined it. "Anything?" I called to Dad, a few minutes later.

"No," he called back, and I could tell that he was now definitely panicking. "Keep looking!"

There was nothing. She'd left no sign at all. She'd … vanished.

*People go missing in this forest all the time.*

"Mum!" I yelled again. "*Muuuuuuuuum!*"

As my bellow was sucked into the black hole of the forest, I heard the song again.

It started out as a thin, wavering note, barely even there. At first I thought it was the wind gathering again but it was pitched higher than that. It rose and rose and then fell a little before getting higher again. Most sound died out here, strangled as soon as the forest got hold of it, but this seemed to pierce the firs with no trouble at all. I still couldn't work out where it was coming from or even how far away it was – it seemed to be all around us.

Dad didn't seem to notice it, but it was all I could hear. The sound filled my head, blocking out everything else. The pitch rose again and I stopped dead, turning around where I stood. There was nothing there, nothing there, nothing there...

Something grabbed my arm. I jerked my head around to find Dad staring at me.

"What are you doing?" he asked. "We've got to find your mother."

"That noise," I said, coughing as I breathed in a cloud of icy snow. "I keep hearing it, at the house and out here. What is it?"

He frowned, letting me go and glancing around us. "What's what?"

"That noise, that ... song!" I said again. "Can't you hear it?"

But it had stopped. I could hear nothing but the sound of Dad's breathing close to my ear.

"It was only the wind in the trees," Dad said. "Help me find Mum. Now!"

I shook myself. The snow was falling harder now. It was being whisked up, too, flurrying off the ground in little knots and eddies as the wind gusted harder.

"Mum!" I yelled, tramping after Dad. "Mum! Where are you?"

Something caught my eye. The growing snowstorm had darkened the mass of firs but as I looked into the shadows beneath their lowest branches, I could see something. A gleam of light.

And I knew. Just like that, I knew exactly where Mum was.

"Dad!" I shouted. He was a few paces ahead of me, still yelling Mum's name. I reached out and snatched a handful of his coat to force him to stop. "Dad!"

He turned but I'd set off before he even had chance to ask what I wanted. I headed towards that little patch of light in the darkness as if I had a map of the forest in my head. I knew that where that light hit the snowy forest floor I would find the stream I'd crossed that first time I came out here. Beyond it was the tangled mess of the old growth forest and that horrible, horrible carved scar. But there would be something else there, too, something that made it worth going back. I knew it.

We emerged from beneath the firs to find the air thick with snow. The sound of the stream trickled and eddied under the frozen grasses, sounding more like summer than winter. I stepped over it and into the wood beyond. It was instantly colder. Here the snow had found its way into every nook and cranny of the uneven trees. The lichen was stiff with ice, stabbing down from the branches like broken shards of pale green glass.

Nothing moved. I stood still for a moment, looking around. The snow kept falling, heavy flakes filling the air like ash, but there was no wind. Without the wind, I wasn't sure I'd be able to find it.

Dad stood beside me, as still as the trees around us. I think he was a bit stunned, the way I had been the first time I'd been here. "Where are we?" he asked. "What is this place? Is this even our plantation?"

"It's the old forest," I muttered, trying to filter him out. "This is what Tomas was so het up about. This is what Erik started hacking down before he upped and left. Mum!" I shouted, raising my voice. "Where are you?"

I scanned the trees in front of me. Back over the stream I'd been convinced I'd recognize the route I'd taken before but the snow had changed everything, or maybe that was the way things worked out here. Maybe nothing was ever the same twice. But then...

A gust of wind blew out of nowhere, sending a flurry of snow so hard into my face that I had to shut my eyes. I wiped away the ice and searched for the movement – and there it was.

"Dad, this way!" I took off, snapping through weeds now frozen as well as matted. I didn't check to see if he was behind me. Ahead I saw the movement again, almost obscured through the growing wind. Then that fluting sound rose around me. It seemed further away this time but managed to be even clearer than before. Haunting, melodic: it was the same verse of that almost-but-not-quite song.

I saw the dying tree before I saw Mum but she was exactly where I knew she'd be. She was kneeling in the same spot I'd seen the boy that first time I'd come out here. She'd taken off her jacket and sweater and her snowshoes, too. She was holding out her arms with her hands palms up to the air, letting the snow fall and melt on her thin fingers. Her head was bowed and bare because she'd also somehow lost her hat. Her long pale hair spilled down over her shoulders in a tangled mass as the snow lost itself in it, leaving droplets of water to hang on the strands. She could almost have been praying, but to what I have no idea.

I dropped to my knees beside her and wrapped my arms round her. She was so cold. "Mum!"

"Ingrid," Dad said, towering over us as he dragged off his jacket and pulled it round her shoulders. "What are you doing?" He didn't wait for an answer, half-lifting, half-pulling her to her feet instead. "We've got to get you home."

"I could hear him," she said, her voice muffled against Dad's chest. "He was calling. He's looking for me. He needs me."

"Who?" I asked, following as Dad struggled to pull her back towards the stream. "Mum? Who was calling you? Mum?"

"Leave it," Dad said gruffly. "We've got to get her back to the house. Help me!"

We left that strange song behind as we made it back over the stream. It faded slowly, getting further and further away. Then, as I thought it was gone for good, I heard something else. It sounded almost like the howl of a wolf. That was fine by me. *Anything but that strange song,* I thought. *Anything but that.*

I wanted to ask Mum what – who – had been calling her. Had she heard that song, too? That must have been what she meant. That sound had started up and she went AWOL, just like that.

So maybe it wasn't a song or an instrument or even a hunting horn.

Maybe it was something else.

Something worse.

The trees roar.
They are angry.
They are angry with us.

*Hurry*, they say, *you must hurry.*
*Payment was ready.*
*Payment was waiting.*
*Listen to the song.*
*Follow the song.*

We move faster, faster.

# Chapter Seventeen

We got Mum into the house. By the time we reached the front door, she seemed to have come back to herself – not completely, but at least there was something in her eyes that I vaguely recognized. She was shivering with cold – so was Dad – and we took her into the living room where the fire had been kept smouldering pretty much constantly since Tomas and the children had left. Dad and I put Mum on the sofa and then Dad stoked the fire while I ran upstairs to find her some blankets. On the way back down I saw Dorothea standing near the covered hole at the bottom of the stairs.

"Could you make some hot chocolate?" I said. "My mum needs to get warm."

The old woman eyed me with complete contempt.

"Please," I said. "Or I can do it myself if you show me where everything is."

She curled her lip and skittered away without

saying anything. I went into the living room, almost too tired to be angry. Almost, but not quite. I figured I'd give Mum the blankets and then go and do exactly what I'd said I would – make the damn hot drinks myself. But as it turned out, I didn't have to. Dorothea turned up a few minutes later with a tray. It crossed my mind that she found making the chocolate for us herself less trouble than having me poking around the kitchen. I'd still never been inside it. That was her domain, like the attic.

Dad gave up the idea of bringing any more wood in from the drying shed. "We won't go out there again, Ingrid," he said. "I should never have taken you out there in the first place."

"We'll just have to ration what we have," he said to me, later that night, once Mum had gone to bed. His face was grey and faded. I realized that he had stubble on his face – he obviously hadn't shaved for a couple of days, which wasn't like him. "If we're careful, we'll be all right. We'll close down most of the rooms, shutter up as many windows as we can against the wind. We can board up some of the external doors, too, if we need to. Just use the main ones. We'll be all right."

"Dad," I said, "seriously, why can't we leave? You said the police would evacuate us. Don't you think we should take that offer and run with it? We can come back next year, can't we? It wouldn't be giving up."

Dad clasped his hands together. "Look," he said. "If it actually gets dangerous to be here, we'll call the police. All right? But I really don't want to do that until and unless it's absolutely necessary. If the story gets around that we can't handle the winter up here, getting reliable labour will be a nightmare. Give this a chance. Help me. Please?"

Well, what could I say to that? Except – "What about Mum?" I asked. "She's really not well."

Dad made a face. "She'll be all right. She just needs quiet. Time to gather her thoughts. She was tired today, that's all. She'll be better tomorrow."

I wasn't convinced but I wasn't the responsible adult, was I? What was I supposed to do? Flat refuse to lift a finger? There were only four of us in that house and apparently right then only two of us were capable of anything resembling sensible behaviour.

I went up to bed. I crawled under my duvet and sleep crowded in on me, making me feel heavy as soon as I hit the mattress. I think that might have been the fastest I've ever fallen asleep in my life.

I woke a little while later to a scratching sound. I lay still and listened. It sounded as though it was at the window. There was another storm blowing outside, so I put it down to that. But the scratching went on and on. Then I realized that it wasn't just at the window. It was inside my room. It was coming from the floor. My heart immediately started banging in my chest, even though I told myself to stay calm. *It's probably just a mouse,* I told myself, although I knew it'd have to be more than one to be making a sound that loud.

I reached out my hand to the lamp on my bedside table. Stretching it through the cold dark felt as if I was holding it out over an abyss. I flicked the switch and yellow light bloomed into the room, making me a little braver. I sat up and peered down over the side of my bed.

There was a tree sprouting through my floor. It had pushed its way between the boards and was growing bit by bit into my room. Then I saw that it wasn't alone. More and more began to claw their way in, their branches *scratch-scratch-scratching* away

185

at the wood as they burst through the floorboards. They grew faster and faster. Then I felt the bed move. They were underneath it, too. There was a creaking, springing sound. I whipped the duvet out of the way and there was a tree ripping its way up through the mattress. I scrambled back against the headboard, gasping and trying to scream to Mum and Dad for help but no matter how hard I tried, I couldn't make any sound. More and more trees were invading the room, splitting the walls and cracking the ceiling as they grew taller and taller, denser and denser. With them they brought the cold and the storm. I could see snow on their branches, feel it in the air, smell it, even. They brought shadows, too, that thick darkness that pooled around their trunks. It spread towards me. I was too terrified to move.

I felt a sharp pain in my side. I looked down to see spindly branches pushing through my belly, opening up my skin like bony fingers. I screamed again but I still couldn't make a sound. I tried to rip myself away but the tree just kept growing, right through me, up and up towards the ceiling, tearing me to shreds as it went. Across what was left of the room I saw something move. A fluid shape shifted out of the shadows. It was a wolf but for some reason it also seemed to be a child, a girl. I tried to work this out as all the time the tree continued to tear me apart. I could see my blood spilling down in a thick river over the duvet on to the floor. I was trying to scream, the pain so huge that bright lights were sparking in my head like grenades going off.

The wolf padded silently across the room towards me and I knew it could smell my blood. Then the creature stopped and it wasn't a wolf any more. It was a girl in a white nightdress.

"Please don't," I tried to beg her. "Please, please don't…"

She opened her mouth in a smile but instead of teeth I saw fangs. Her eyes were yellow.

Then I woke up again, screaming louder than I ever had in my life.

# Chapter Eighteen

The next day, Dad and I went out to the woodshed closer to the house, the one beside the barn full of our ruined equipment. The wind tore around us, the trees whispered and writhed. It wasn't snowing but that didn't mean there wasn't still plenty of snow. I thought back to that morning after the first snowfall, how it had hardly even come over the tread of my boots. Now it reached to my knees, or it would have if I'd tried stepping on it in my normal footwear. It was impossible to go anywhere outside the house without snowshoes. The drifts were too deep.

*It's just snow,* I kept telling myself, over and over, as Dad and I trudged slowly out to the sheds, dragging a sled behind us because there was no way a wheelbarrow was going to be any use at all. *It's just weather. It's not doing it deliberately. It's not out to get us. Stop being crazy. You're just tired, that's all.*

I was definitely very tired. I hadn't slept at all

since I'd woken from that nightmare. I kept telling myself that's what it had been, but it had felt like more than that. It still did, even hours later. My side hurt. Right where those spindly branches had ripped out my guts, I had a horrible, gnawing pain, as if something inside me was trying to work its way out through my skin. I kept telling myself that the pain wasn't really there. But it was. It was.

As we got to the barn I looked up and saw the burn marks that had clawed their way up its outside and for the first time in ages I thought about those photographs I'd found. The image in the Polaroid of this burned barn came back to me with a vengeance, along with everything else. The dying tree. The song I kept hearing that could pierce right through the forest. Mum wandering off, as though she was following it.

I wondered what would have happened if I hadn't had that sudden realization about where she'd be. Would we have found her at all? If we hadn't, would something else have instead? I kept thinking about that girl from my dream, about the tearing, awful horror of those trees invading my room. In my head it all started joining together, one big blur of scary stuff that I couldn't even think clearly about, let alone explain. I was so tired.

*People go missing in this forest all the time.*

Dorothea's voice echoed in my head so clearly that I looked over my shoulder in case she'd followed us. But there was only Dad and me and a big pile of butchered trees.

"We'll need to be careful about what we use from now on," Dad was saying. "So we'll cut these larger logs in half with a chainsaw."

I tried to concentrate on what he was saying but my mind kept wandering. Part of me wanted to tell him about my nightmare. I wanted to say, "Hey, can we leave this until another day? Because right now I don't think I can deal with being out here with the trees, even the dead ones." But I couldn't say that, could I? He'd think I was losing my mind. Hell, *I* thought I was losing my mind. Anyway, we'd already got all the way out to the barn. Better to get it over with, right? The quicker I started, the sooner it'd be over and I'd be back inside the house.

*Just a few hours,* I told myself. *Get on with it and get it done.*

I followed Dad into the middle barn. It was

impossible not to look at the tatters of rubber hanging from the wheels of our ruined equipment. It was also impossible not to think they looked a lot like how my skin had ended up in that nightmare, as if they'd been ripped apart by the same thing.

I blinked and forced myself to look away. *Stop it,* I told myself, again. *It was only a dream. You know it was. Trees can't tear anything into pieces. Children don't look normal one minute and like wolves the next. They don't have fangs and claws.*

Dad gave me a chainsaw and a pair of safety glasses.

He tapped the saw. "You ever used one of these before?"

I shook my head. The chainsaw was heavy. I could feel my arms protesting as I followed him back into the woodshed next door. I could lift it though. Just about.

"I'll do the first few with you, then I'll go back to the house, check on your mum and start boarding up the windows," he said. "Once you've got enough to fill a sled, bring it inside – we'll keep an extra stock next to the big fireplace in the living room from now on. You'll be fine as long as you're careful

191

and concentrate. I wouldn't ask you to do this if I didn't have to and I didn't think you could handle it. All right?"

I nodded numbly, then watched as Dad showed me how to use the saw. The chain tore into the white flesh of the wood, churning it into mush. I was kind of mesmerized by it until it was my turn to try. The vibration of the machine shuddered up my arms and into my jaw, chattering my teeth and making my gut ache even more.

Dad watched me for a while, then gave me a nod and left me there. I stopped sawing long enough to take out my iPod and find something really loud to stuff into my ears. It drowned out the sound of the saw as well as the dull, circular track of my thoughts. Then I started sawing. I cut and I cut and I cut, my muscles burning and my ears throbbing.

*Just keep going. Just keep going. Just keep going…*

I'd got the first load of wood into the sled and was starting to struggle back to the house when I saw it. It wasn't much – a tiny gleam in the blue-black light. Four spatters of hot red sinking into a snow drift about three metres from the barn. I stared at it for a second. Then I turned off my iPod and took my earphones out.

Without the music, I could hear the trees. *Whoo-oooosh*, they whispered in that constant wind-blown roar, with the occasional little *whump-whump-whump* of laughter thrown in.

I got closer. Red drops on white snow. Blood. I froze. Right then it was like I was looking at the last of those Polaroids I'd been thinking about earlier. *Don't be an idiot*, I told myself. *You think that picture is the only time there has ever been blood on the snow out here? Get a grip.*

I looked around. There was too much light to use a torch and yet it was too gloomy not to squint. What really freaked me out was that there were no signs of any tracks except for Dad's and mine. Our snowshoes showed the route we had taken to and from the house, but other than that – and those blobs of red – the snow all around was pristine. I checked myself – even though I was wearing thick work gloves, for a second I wondered if one of them had ripped and I'd cut myself without feeling it, but they were fine. I took one off and touched my face, in case I'd had a nosebleed or something, but there was nothing. My legs were fine, too.

It wasn't until I looked closer that I saw the blood wasn't an isolated spatter. It was a trail. After the first few drops, there was a gap of a metre. Then, up on one of the deeper drifts, there was another little huddle of blood and then, a few metres after that, another. It led back behind the barn and away into the firs. I know that because I followed it. I didn't want to. My heart was pounding and I felt sick. What I wanted to do was go back to the house as fast as I could, slam the door and never leave it again. But what I did was follow that horrible trail right up and into the firs. I had to. I don't think I had a choice.

I was so tired but something in me was determined to follow that blood. So I did. I stumbled and clawed my way into the forest. It was cold but I didn't really notice that at the time. I don't remember noticing anything but the blood. For once I didn't even really notice the trees.

I kept going until I didn't need to any more. I didn't need to because what had been leaving the blood trail had stopped. I knew that because it was still lying there, or at least its body was. Bits of it, anyway. It was – had been – an elk. A massive bull by the look of its antlers, which were about the only thing that whatever had hunted it hadn't had a go at eating. Everything else had been torn to shreds. Think of the last time you saw road kill – what it would have looked like if you hadn't been too grossed out to look as your car sailed safely past. Now think of that times one hundred, because elk are *big*.

Staring at the carcass, I had another flashback. Not to the photographs this time, or even to my dream, but to Alisa, lying in the basement. I thought of her broken leg, the jagged white bone sticking through her split skin. But this was much worse. Something had ripped out this thing's stomach and wallowed in it. The elk's entrails had been spread all over the place, radiating from it like a kid's drawing of the sun's rays. The blood wasn't only blood, it was real gore – mixed with chunks of skin and gut and gobbets of fat and God only knew what else. This mess had melted the snow as it touched down, so that there were little rivulets sunk into the crusted white. They spread out from the carcass in ridges and whorls and tiny gullies, like veins that had been unwound and were being sucked towards the trees.

The blood was still glistening against the snow,

which meant the carnage couldn't have happened that long before. How could I not have heard anything? Not even Opeth could have blocked out the sound of that thing dying. I looked around, suddenly afraid that I'd interrupted the kill and I was next on the menu. But there was nothing. No sign of any other creature at all. *How?* My brain screamed at me. *How can there be no other sign?* This thing was lying under the trees, its guts ripped apart, its eyes gouged out, every piece of hide ripped and splattered with blood and gristle. How could that happen without whatever did it leaving a trace? The creature responsible had run off. So there should have been another trail, right? A dozen other trails – there should have been trampled, bloody snow where the killer had charged back into the forest. But there was nothing.

Except that then there was.

It slid silently into the periphery of my vision and stood a little way to my left, in the darkness beyond the carcass. It separated itself from the trees too deliberately to be a shadow and I knew without even looking that it wasn't anything good. Fear prickled along my spine as I stood there, staring at the mess that had once been a living thing while all the time there was this other thing there, just *there*, waiting for me to look at it. I froze, as if I could wait it out, or it might wander off of its own accord if I didn't move. But all the while I knew that wasn't going to happen.

It wanted me to turn. It wanted me to look at it.

I didn't want to, any more than I'd wanted to follow the trail of blood. But still, I did. Slowly, I turned to look. I clenched my hands so tightly that the fabric of my gloves ground itself into the skin of my palms. I was trying not to shake but every part of me was quivering with fear.

It was a child. A girl of about ten, maybe. She was standing ankle deep in snow, wearing what looked like an old-fashioned nightdress. It was a grubby white, as though it hadn't been washed for a while, or maybe it had been washed too much. Her hair was long and fell in tangled waves almost down to her waist. Her arms were hanging limply at her sides, her hands hidden by red gloves.

It was the girl from my dream. I recognized her, in that weird way that in dreams you recognize things even though they're different to how they are in reality. I knew it was her. I knew it, even though her eyes weren't yellow this time. Now they were pools of bottomless black.

Her fingers twitched and something fell from them, a trickle of liquid dark dripping into the snow beside her feet.

I stared at the delicate red pattern that was dotting itself into the white.

It was blood. Her hands were covered in it. What I'd assumed were gloves was actually a thick coating of gore.

The girl smiled. It was a slow, deliberate gesture and as her mouth opened it revealed two rows of fangs. Her gums and teeth were streaked with blood. It dripped from her canines, slipping over her thin white lips to run down her chin.

I must have screamed, though I can't remember it. I know I turned and ran, except that you can't run in snowshoes. The best you can do is a shuffle slightly quicker than walking. But I tried, even though I knew it was useless. I could feel her behind me, a movement of air as she came after me, the sound of breathing, panting, snarling. She was *so fast*.

I stumbled over the snow. The lowest branches

of the firs scraped at me, scratching my hands and face, stabbing at me as I pushed through them. I expected to feel those teeth sink into my neck as she brought me to the ground. She'd killed the elk and now she was hunting something else. Now she was hunting me.

Then, there it was. The song, or call, or hunting horn, whatever it was. It rose around me like the wind and I honestly thought that was it. I thought I was dead. It was telling her to attack and—

*BANG!*

The sound of the gunshot knocked me off my feet. I crashed into the snow face first, the impact pushing all the air out of my lungs. My head cracked against the bark of the closest tree and I think I blacked out for a second, because the next thing I knew Dad was beside me, shaking my shoulder.

I'd scrambled up on my knees before he managed to stop me.

"Hey," he said, "take it easy. Are you all right?"

I spun round, flailing in the snow, looking behind me. "Where is she?" I gasped. "Did you shoot her?"

"Don't think I hit her," Dad said, still trying to check me over. "She's gone."

I turned back again, grabbing Dad's jacket. "But you saw her? You did?"

Dad frowned, holding me still and checking my head. "Yes, I saw her. Although I think it might have been male, not female."

I was still gasping for air. I couldn't understand what he meant. "What?"

"The wolf. I think it might have been male, not female. Unless it's got pups around here somewhere. I guess that might make a female that aggressive. Either way, in future we shouldn't come out here alone, or without this." He indicated the shotgun in his hand. "What were you doing out here anyway? You're supposed to be in the woodshed."

"Wolf?" I gasped. "What wolf? The girl, Dad. Didn't you see the girl?"

Dad frowned and touched my forehead. "How hard did you hit your head? Come on, let's—"

I fell back into the snow, scrabbling at my clothes as Dad tried to hold me still. I think he thought I was having a fit. I pushed his hands away and pulled up my top, the freezing air biting at my skin.

I looked down at myself. There was blood pouring out of a gash below my lowest right rib.

Dad swore and put his hand over the wound. "You must have fallen on a sharp tree branch," he said. "Come on, can you stand? We've got to get you back to the house." He took my hand, glove and all, and pressed it where his had been a moment earlier. "Put pressure on it. I don't know how deep it is."

He pulled me up, both arms around me to keep me upright as we staggered back towards the house. My legs weren't working properly – I was shaking too much.

I looked down at the cut in my side. In fact, there wasn't only one. There were three, next to each other, all in a jagged line. It didn't look like something a tree branch would do.

It looked like a claw mark.

The forest is laughing.
*They think they can save themselves from you,*
it whispers. *They cannot.*
*Not now you are here.*

We weave between the trees,
anger growing like fire.
*We want them*, we say.
*We want them now.*

# Chapter Nineteen

I didn't stop shaking for a long time, even once we were back at the house. I couldn't understand what was happening. Had it all been in my head? Was I going completely insane? How could Dad have seen a wolf out there when I had seen a little girl?

"I want to see Mum," I said to Dad as he patched me up, my teeth chattering.

Dad patted my shoulder. "Sure. That's probably a good idea. Why don't you take her up some lunch? Dorothea's laid some out for us and I don't think your mum's eaten yet. Sit and have a chat. That'll probably do you both good. Only ... try not to worry her, all right? Try not to tell her anything about what happened out there. It won't do her – or you – any good. And it can wait, can't it? Until she's better?"

I nodded, my teeth still chattering.

I was shaking as I went upstairs with food for both of us. I kept struggling not to let it slide off the plates as I carried them. Something in me wouldn't or couldn't calm down. I kept seeing that girl, and now I couldn't work out what had been in my nightmare and what I'd seen out there in the snow. The cut in my side had stopped bleeding, but it still hurt. And I knew – I knew that it was exactly where the tree in my dream had torn its way into my flesh. That couldn't be a coincidence. Or could it? I tried to remember if a branch had hit me right there in the side as I'd tried to get away. Maybe it had. But then why weren't my clothes torn?

I tried to stop thinking about it all. I tried to concentrate on putting one foot in front of the other and not dropping the plates in my hand and stopping my teeth from chattering. And I tried to work out what I was going to say to Mum.

I couldn't tell her about the dream or the girl I thought I'd seen in the woods, or even the wolf. I had to find something completely harmless. Something she might respond to. How ridiculous is that, trying to come up with a way to break the ice with your own mother? They never teach you this at school. No one ever says, "Right – today we're going to learn how to deal with parental breakdown." How was I supposed to know what to *do*?

When I got to the end of the corridor, I saw that the door to my parents' room was ajar. As I got nearer I could hear voices. At first I thought it was just Mum, talking to herself, but then I got close enough to see through the gap.

It was Dorothea.

Mum was sitting on the edge of the bed with her head bowed. Dorothea was standing in front of her with her hands on her hips. She was talking too quietly for me to hear what she was saying from where I was but Mum was nodding. It was an odd, jerky movement that rocked her back and forth on the mattress every time her head moved.

I shouldered open the door. Dorothea looked up at me but Mum carried on staring at the floor.

"What are you doing in here?" I demanded.

Dorothea stepped away from Mum and shrugged. "Checking on the mistress."

"Did my dad ask you to do that?" The housekeeper stared at me with blank eyes but didn't answer. "What were you saying to her?"

"I was asking if she wanted something to eat."

I looked at my mother. She had lifted her head and

was staring out of the window at the endless trees beyond. The fingers of her left hand were scratching at her right wrist.

"I don't believe you," I said. "What were you really saying?"

Dorothea stared at me for another moment and then skittered right past me with her weird little walk.

"Stay away from my mother," I said to her back. "We'll look after her. Understand? Stay away."

She didn't even acknowledge that I'd spoken. I kicked the door shut behind her. Mum was still staring out of the window.

"Mum?" I said. "I've brought you some food."

I don't think she knew who I was at first. She looked at me like I were a stranger who had wandered into her room by accident. It scared me. I mean, if your own mother doesn't know who you are, what does that say about you?

Her absent look passed though, after a moment. I saw the shadow leaving her eyes and she even managed a watery smile. She stood up and stretched her hands out to me for a moment. I would have reached out to her, too, but I still had the plates and cutlery in my hands, so I looked around for somewhere to put them down and settled on the dressing table.

"You should eat something," I told her, suddenly aware that she was looking thinner as well as sadder, almost as if someone had tipped her up and emptied a bit of her out. Her cheekbones were sharper, her cheeks more hollow. Her eyes looked bigger than normal, too. I didn't like it. She didn't look like my mother, she looked like someone doing a pretty good impression of her.

Mum looked at the plate. I don't think she'd noticed it until then. "I'm not really hungry."

"Still ... you should."

"Maybe later."

There was an awkward pause as I tried to work out what else to say. I looked around the room and wondered what she did all day, stuck in here on her own. There weren't any books anywhere, so I said, "Maybe I could show you where the library is? It's huge – you'd like it," but even as I said it I remembered Dad had tried already. "Or – or I could bring you something to read, if you like?"

She smiled again, or at least I think that's what

she was doing. It was a vague tightening of her jaw but her attention was already wandering. She kept glancing back towards the window.

"Mum? Would that be good? If I brought you some books?"

"You don't need to worry about me," she said suddenly. "He'll keep me company."

"But Dad's worried about you, I can tell," I said. "I am, too."

"You don't need to worry," she repeated, her voice a bit distant and dreamy. "We'll get to know each other. I just need to show him the way back. I know that now."

Something icy planted itself at the top of my spine and began to slowly work its way down. It took me a moment to say anything and when I did, my voice came out in a croak. "Who? Did Dorothea tell you something? What did she say?"

Mum looked at me again. She looked old. "I'm tired," she said.

"OK. Will you eat something? Please?" She'd already turned away. "Mum?"

Her face was turned towards the window and she didn't answer. She was scratching her wrist again, the other one this time. I stood there for a few minutes, wondering what to do. Then I went back downstairs.

Dad was sitting at our dinner table, eating quickly. He looked up when I came in.

"Feeling any better?" he asked.

I opened my mouth to say something but I couldn't work out where to start.

Dad frowned. "What's wrong?"

"I don't think Mum's going to eat what I took her."

He stared down at his plate for a moment and then nodded. "I'll go up in a minute. See if I can persuade her."

Another silence.

"She's really not well," I said, into the stale air between us.

"No, she's not."

"We should call a doctor."

Dad sighed and stood up. "That's the one thing she doesn't want."

I frowned. "What do you mean?"

Dad rubbed his thumb and forefinger over the bridge of his nose. He looked weary. "Look," he said. "She's always had a fear of doctors. Especially

… especially for this kind of thing."

By 'this kind of thing', I assume he meant mental health. I guess he was still part of that generation where you just don't talk about it. Yeah, because that's really healthy. Nothing bad ever happened to anyone because of that attitude, right?

"She wants peace and quiet," he went on. "That's all. That's what she keeps telling me. She'll be fine as long as she can just have some peace, quiet and sleep. We'll look after her. Nothing can hurt her up here, can it?" He laughed slightly but he sounded as tired as he looked. "It's not as if there's anyone else here but us, is there?"

I thought about the girl in the forest and about the boy who hadn't been on the bus and about Dorothea. But the more I thought, the less sure I was about anything. Dad's face was so grey, so tight with stress. He wouldn't believe me if I told him what I'd seen – who would? I didn't have any way to prove it, either. He'd think I was losing it, too. Like Mum.

"I really think we should leave," I said. "Please, Dad. Please, let's just go."

Dad looked up at me. "Your mother wants to stay," he said. "I asked her last night and she said

211

she wants to stay. She said—" He looked down at the table again and drummed his fingers against the white cloth that covered it. "She said she has to."

Dad obviously thought that was the end of the discussion. He got up, his food half-finished.

"I'll go and check on your mother," he said. "Then I've got some more shutters to fix up. I could use your help."

I nodded and waited until he'd gone. I left enough time to be sure that he'd made it upstairs. Then I went into the hallway for a moment, listening in case he came back quickly, but all I could hear was the fresh blizzard that had risen outside. I went to the phone in the entrance hall. Our address book from Stockholm lay next to it and I flicked to the number of our old doctor back home. I stared at the number for a while. Then I dialled it.

"Please," I said, to the receptionist through the bad crackle on the line. "I just need to talk to her. It'll only take a few minutes. It's important. Please."

The woman on the other end sighed. "Doctor Nilstrom has a full roster of patients. You really should make a proper appointment and come in personally. We don't do telephone consultations."

"I'm not in Stockholm," I said, "I'm in the middle of nowhere in northern Sweden. We're snowed in and I'm worried that my mother's going mad. I just need to talk to the doctor. *Please.*"

There was a pause. "Wait a moment," said the woman's voice and then both the crackle and her were replaced by tinny hold music. I waited for an age and then she was back. "Hello?"

"Yes? Can I talk to the doctor?"

"I'm sorry," said the receptionist. "But Doctor Nilstrom can't discuss your mother's medical needs with you. She's welcome to call herself, if she likes."

"She won't," I said, a feeling of hopelessness washing over me. "I know she won't."

"Well, the doctor says that the other alternative is for you and your father to contact the local psychiatric service up there. If you are really concerned and think she is in danger of harming herself or someone else, then there are measures that can be taken. I can give you the number now. Are you ready?"

To be honest, I'd stopped listening after the word 'measures'. Mum didn't need locking up and that's what they were talking about, right? Even the thought made me feel sick. She wasn't crazy like that. She couldn't be. She was the most level-headed person I knew. Like Dad had said, she probably just needed peace and quiet. And anyway, she wasn't going to hurt herself, was she? She definitely wouldn't hurt anyone else. We could look after her, Dad and me. If going back to Stockholm meant she'd be taken away, maybe it wasn't such a good idea after all.

The receptionist reeled off the number but I wasn't listening. I thanked her and put the phone down, just in time to hear Dad's footsteps overhead.

# Chapter Twenty

I spent the rest of the evening helping Dad, which seemed to mean sealing ourselves in. All the windows had fitted metal plates that could be screwed over them from the inside, so I held them in place while Dad drove in the bolts. By the time we had finished, the windows downstairs were covered. It felt as though we had locked ourselves inside a tomb. I should have been freaked out but instead, it made me feel safe. Neither Dad nor I said much as we worked. I should have told him about the elk and the girl I thought I'd seen, but I couldn't work out how without sounding completely insane. The more I thought about it, the more I decided I must have imagined her. That the thing that had chased me really had just been a wolf. You know, one of the ones that were supposed to be more afraid of us than we were of them. Yeah, right.

It was after midnight when we finally finished

and I went upstairs to bed. My body was tired but my mind was nowhere near sleep. I kept thinking about the girl, standing there in the snow with blood dripping from her fingers. The slashes in my side were hurting, despite the painkillers I'd taken. The wind screamed around the walls, rattling the window frames like it was trying to find a way in. Dad hadn't mentioned boarding up the windows on this floor but I hoped that was the next task. It would mean I wouldn't be able to see the trees outside, for a start. I was sick of the forest and scared of what it was doing to us. I tried to avoid looking out at all as I went over to pull the curtains shut.

I could hear the firs rustling in the wind outside, restlessly moving against each other. I kept my eyes on the floor. It seemed that they were nearer the house, as if the edge of the forest had taken a collective step closer, crowding in, surrounding us so that we wouldn't be able to get out. I had this sudden, horrible idea that if I looked up at the window I would see a mass of branches pressed against the glass – that it wasn't the wind trying to find a way in but the firs themselves – my nightmare become a reality.

I crawled into bed and pulled the duvet over my

head. I lay there for what felt like hours, listening to the screech and scrape of the trees outside and wondering what else was out there among them. I kept tossing and turning. I didn't think I'd sleep at all but I must have, at least a little, because when I next looked at my watch it was after 3 a.m. The trees were still moving outside and even though I was still tired I didn't think I was going to go to sleep again. I went back to thinking about what I thought I'd seen in the forest, about how Mum was falling apart, wondering if the same thing was happening to me. I thought about how long we were going to be trapped here for, in this tomb of a house. In the end I decided to get up.

I went back to the office where I'd found the photographs. I'd been in there earlier when Dad and I had shuttered the windows but I'd been so out of it that I hadn't even really looked at the desk. I half expected to find that they had disappeared. I wouldn't have been surprised if Dorothea had gathered them up. But no, everything was exactly as I'd left it when Alisa's accident had happened, even the photographs that had fallen to the floor.

I stood at the desk, looking down at the Polaroids

lying on top of it. "Hello, Erik," I said to the man in the selfies.

I pulled out the chair and gathered up the old black-and-whites from the floor. One of them had fallen face down and for the first time I realized that it had something written on the back of it. I picked up the photograph and looked at the scrawled handwriting. I was pretty sure that whoever had written it was the same person who had also written on the back of the Polaroids – the writing looked similar. So that had to have been Erik himself, right?

*Girl, aged about 7,* said the note. *Disappeared from Storaskogen in 1949.*

A weird, tight feeling pulled at my chest as I turned over the rest of the pictures.

*Boy, aged around 10,* said the next one. *Last mentioned at Storaskogen in 1957. Cannot trace without name.*

*Girl, aged around 12. Name unknown. Went missing in 1979. Dead?*

I stared at the words as though I might force them to change into something else but of course they didn't.

*People go missing in this forest all the time.*

218

Dorothea's voice whispered in the back of my mind, like the hollow whooshing of the wind in the trees outside. I felt numb. I got up slowly, with the photographs still in my hand. I picked up the Polaroids, too. Then I laid everything out on the desk in a line.

*There has to be a reasonable explanation*, I told myself. If these kids really had gone missing, it was years ago. Someone must have investigated, right? Someone must know what had happened to them.

I sat down on the chair and concentrated on the faces in the black-and-white pictures – not only on the family themselves and the kids that had apparently gone missing but the rest of the household, too. All those servants who had once lived here. Where were they now? Sure, some of them would be pretty old but they couldn't all be dead. As I looked at each of the pictures one after another, I realized something. Several of the faces were repeated from one photograph to the next. Even though the families who owned the place had changed, clearly they had kept on some of the servants. I guess that made sense – they'd know how the place worked, after all. Why train new staff when the old ones

219

already knew what they were doing?

As I looked at those pictures I realized something else. I recognized one of the faces. Sure, she was older now, wizened and bent over – but it was definitely her.

Dorothea was in every one of these photographs.

I put them in date order according to the notes on the backs and there she was, getting older as the decades went by. In the first one – the one marked as 1949 – she actually looked young. She can't have been much older than me in that picture – eighteen, maybe? – but she still wasn't wearing even the trace of a smile. I guess the bitterness sunk in early and never left.

There is no sign of payment.
Our anger grows.
*We are being cheated*, we tell the trees.
*They will not settle their debts.*

*They will*, whispers the forest.
*They have no choice.*
*Do you remember?*

We do.

# Chapter Twenty-One

I went into the kitchen. I didn't really want to, but it seemed to me that if I wanted answers, Dorothea was the one to give them to me, whether that was what she or I wanted. She'd known those kids. She'd lived through all of them going missing – *People go missing in this forest all the time* – so she had to know something about what had happened, didn't she?

I'd kind of assumed that the kitchen was immediately beyond the door that led out of the breakfast room but I was wrong. That door opened on to a narrow passageway, just wide enough for a person to walk down carrying a tray. I hesitated on the threshold. Something about that corridor made me nervous. There were no windows. The only light was a bare bulb hanging from the low ceiling. I switched it on and it flickered slightly as I passed under it, throwing uneven shadows against the tattered walls.

There was nothing notable about the door at the other end except that the handle had been worn so smooth that when I tried to turn it, my fingers found it hard to grip. At least when it did turn, it was quiet. The door swung inwards into darkness and a smell of cooking – fat, sausages and about a million other things I couldn't quite identify. The nerves in my stomach had wound themselves so tight that the smell made me feel sick.

I'd expected her to be there. Sure, it was still only just five in the morning but didn't people in her profession get up at stupid hours to light fires and things? She always had breakfast ready and waiting for us on the dot of seven so she had to be up before that, at least. But the room was empty.

I looked around. There was a large wooden table right in the centre. It was cluttered with rolling pins, pots of utensils, bread boards, loaf tins. In the middle was a cleared space that was obviously what Dorothea used for preparation. Once, back when time was dawning and evolution was still sorting out whether we'd be better off with feathers or fingers, the whole table had probably been needed but now there were only four of us in the house.

To my left and right, snug up against the walls, were large dressers, their top halves full of stacked crockery, their bottom halves solid chests of drawers and cupboards.

The kitchen was a lot smaller than I'd been expecting. It would have fitted inside my bedroom. I thought about Dorothea spending so much time here – which she obviously did, because there was an old wooden rocking chair and a small side table set beside the large fireplace at the back of the room. On the table was a silver teapot and a single battered silver cup. I could imagine her sitting there in this dim, airless room, rocking and rocking and speaking to no one all day.

That's when I noticed what was on top of the fireplace. The mantel had been made from a single piece of wood that looked as old as Dorothea herself. It was stacked with odds and ends – sticks of candle half-melted in their holders like horror-film props, old paperback books with the pages dry and curled, what seemed to be a carved whalebone (at least, I hoped it was a whalebone), that kind of thing.

And … a photograph. There was a single black-and-white photograph propped up at one end.

I moved closer, skirting the edge of the table and making my way around one of those massive old tea trolleys with wheels. The first thing I noticed about the picture was that it was very similar to the ones of Storaskogen I'd just been looking at. Yet another household was lined up in that strange monotone summer sunshine outside the main house doors. There was the man of the house – another big, strapping specimen with a 'mine, all mine' expression on his face. This time, though, the photograph seemed only to be of the master and his staff, because he was surrounded by uniformed servants. My first thought was that maybe he hadn't had a family. Then I realized that what I was looking at was only part of the photograph. Most of it had been folded over on itself. It must have been done years ago – the crease was so firm that I couldn't unfold it without risking tearing the picture in two. I had to turn the photograph over to see the rest.

There was a woman and a boy in the photograph who, from their outfits, obviously weren't servants. The fold had cut them out of the picture.

The fold had been positioned to slice right through

the boy so that his face was barely visible. And his mother … that was even worse. Someone had scratched out her face, leaving nothing but a halo of yellowing paper where it should have been.

I tried to focus on the boy but it was hard to make out what he looked like because of the fold. I turned the photograph back over again and looked at the people that Dorothea *had* wanted to look at. As I peered closer, I could see her. She was in this photograph too, younger than she had been in the earliest of the others – she looked even younger than me, so maybe fifteen, something like that. She was standing right at her master's left elbow, so small that she barely reached to his shoulder. She wasn't looking at the camera. She was looking up at him with an adoring look on her face. And she was smiling.

The door opened behind me. I spun around to see Dorothea. It took her a second to realize what she was seeing and then the fury descended. It was like a curtain coming down. A very heavy, very red, curtain.

"You!" hissed Dorothea. "Get out! Get out, get out, get out!"

Her gaze fell on the photograph in my hand

and she lunged forwards, trying to grab it. I took a step backwards and held it up over my head, out of her reach.

"I want to talk to you, that's all," I said as she missed the photograph and clattered against the table, upending a pot of utensils. They crashed and rumbled as they rolled around and fell to the floor.

"No right!" she screamed. "You've no right to come in here!"

She was still trying to grab at the photograph. In a way it was kind of tragically pathetic. There was a part of me that wanted to laugh but I think that was an involuntary reaction. Shock, probably. Or terror. But I was determined to find out what I needed to know so I forced myself not to dodge past her and run for the door.

"I just need some information, that's all!" I pointed to the photograph. "This boy – he went missing, didn't he? He went missing like all the others, didn't he?"

She stopped suddenly, puffing heavily, her bony chest heaving up and down. She looked at me with another one of her poisonous glares. I tried to ignore it.

"You know what happened to them, don't you? I want to know, that's all."

Dorothea's gaze dropped to the picture again. "The photograph is *mine*." Her voice was full of venom.

I held out the photograph to her, my hand shaking a little. She snatched it from me and held it in both hands. Her wizened thumb stroked over the image of the man who must have been her master. It occurred to me he might have been her master in more ways than one. She must have been so young when she came here and that would explain the slashed-out face of his wife in the picture, wouldn't it?

"What was the boy's name, Dorothea? Tell me about him."

Dorothea suddenly hawked. For a second I thought she was going to spit at me but instead she whipped her head around and fired a projectile of phlegm into the fireplace. She didn't turn her head back straight away. There was a weird moment of calm.

"I don't remember," she said shortly. "It's too long ago."

"If that was true, you wouldn't remember who

228

else is in that photograph," I said, "but you do. Don't you?" I pointed at it, to the main man, standing in front of all he commanded like he was king of the world. "Him, for instance. You remember *him*, don't you, Dorothea? That's why you've got his photograph here, isn't it?"

She eyed me with what I was pretty sure was pure hate.

"I don't care about any of that," I said again. "Really, I don't. I want to know what happened to this boy. How did he die?"

Dorothea blinked slowly. "He's not dead. Neither is she."

Something cold wrapped around my heart. An image flashed into my head, of that girl in the woods, in my room. "She?" I managed to croak.

Dorothea was still looking at the photograph. Her thumb rubbed over the space where her master's wife's face had once been. Relief exploded in my chest like a firework. She wasn't talking about the girl. Of course she wasn't. She meant the boy's mother.

"So he didn't die," I said, and I could hear the relief bubbling through my voice as I said it. "So they –

what? They left? His mother took him and left?"

She carried on staring at the photograph clutched between her fingers. "There are worse things than death," she said. "Better for us. Worse for them."

I swallowed. My heart started to pound. "What? What do you mean?"

The look she gave me could have sliced raw meat.

"Get out of my kitchen."

"No. Not until you tell me what happened to them," I said. "Who are they? What are their names?" I thought I could look them up, somehow. Find out where they went, maybe. But Dorothea was steely-faced.

"I don't remember."

"You're lying," I said. "You know exactly who they are. Why won't you tell me? Tell me, or I swear I'll…"

"You'll what?" she sneered, taking a step closer. As she moved I saw the gleam of one of the knives rising slightly out of the knifeblock on the table behind her. In a flash I thought of the violent slashes that had removed the mother's face in the picture. I stepped back.

"That's right – run," she hissed, her voice snide,

"foolish child. Thinking you mean something. Thinking you're *important*."

I forced myself to stay still. When I spoke, I was quite proud that my voice didn't shake. "I want to know who they are and what happened to them. All of them. Everyone who's ever gone missing from this place."

Her lips twisted in a demonic sneer. "Never. I will never speak their names. They will never hear them again. They are what they will always be."

Yes, I did indeed realize that she was speaking about them in the present tense. It made me think of Tomas's kids, the ones who had been making the same call I'd heard out in the woods. It was the sound the ghosts made, isn't that what they'd said? The ghosts in the forest.

I swallowed, hard. "What do you mean?" I asked. "What are they? Ghosts?"

She made a sound in her throat, like she was going to spit again, but didn't. "*Ghosts*," she repeated, in disgust. "They are the forest. They are varulv."

"Varulv?" I repeated, the sick feeling I'd had when I'd entered the kitchen returning with a vengeance. "They're … wolves?"

She looked at me scornfully. "Not wolves. *Varulv.*"

Then, before I had a chance to react, she flung herself forwards and pushed me. She had far more strength than I expected. I fell backwards against the wall. My head hit the mantelpiece hard, striking it with a heavy clunk.

"Get out," Dorothea said. "Get out, get out. GET OUT."

# Chapter Twenty-Two

I ran. I scrabbled at the door handle, wrenching it open and then rushing back down the passageway. When I got to the dining room I slammed the door shut and leaned against it. I listened to see if Dorothea had come after me but she hadn't. My heart was banging in my chest. I still felt sick. It wasn't only because Dorothea had scared me – I couldn't work out what any of it meant. Had anything she'd said made sense? Erik's notes on the photographs hadn't mentioned anything about the children's mothers going missing. But wouldn't it explain everything if all they had done was get tired of living with their piggish husbands in this miserable place and taken their children to live somewhere else?

But that wasn't what Dorothea was saying had happened, was it? "They are the forest," she'd said. What the hell did *that* mean?

*Varulv.* The word floated around my mind like

a ghost itself. Tomas had said it was a local word for wolf but that didn't fit with what Dorothea had said. Part of me wanted to go back to my room, get into bed, pull the covers over my head and stay there but a bigger part wanted to know what the hell was going on. Since I couldn't look anything up online and there wasn't anyone to ask, I was going to have to go old school. I headed for the library, checking every few steps to make sure Dorothea wasn't behind me. I would gladly go for the rest of my life without having to see her again.

By the time I reached the library my heart rate had steadied a bit but the nausea was still there. Everything was churning around and around – in my head, in my gut. I stood inside the door for a few minutes, taking in the seemingly endless rows of books and trying to work out where to start. The shelves went right up to the ceiling. There were a couple of those long ladders standing against the cases so that you could reach the upper levels. Most of the volumes looked as old as the ones in the study – bound in cloth and leather, in reds and greens and faded blues. I went to the shelf nearest to me and pulled one out at random as a starting point.

It was an old classic novel, a copy of Lagerkvist's *Ångest*, which wasn't going to be much use in the circumstances. I put it back and went along the shelves, trying to work out what the order was. After a while I worked out that fiction was on one side and non-fiction was on the other.

Concentrating on the non-fiction section, I kept pulling out books here and there, looking for an encyclopaedia. There had to be one. I thought there was probably a copy of every book ever published in Swedish in this room. I had climbed halfway up one of the rickety old ladders before I found it – the first in a multi-volume set. I worked my way along the shelf towards the tome that would have 'V'. When I finally found and reached for it, I noticed that it was pushed in a fraction more than the others. Not by much – maybe a centimetre, that was all. But it was definitely out of place. It was chunky, bound in dull red leather. I pulled it out, twisting on the ladder to hold it in both hands – it weighed a ton.

I struggled back down the steps and elbowed a small pile of books off the nearest table before plonking it down. I flipped to the back first to look in the index – sure enough, there was an entry under

*Varulv.* As I was busy finding the right page, I saw a piece of paper sticking a little way out of the top of the book, as if someone had marked a page. The paper looked like it had been torn out of a lined notepad. The thing that creeped me out, though, was where it was in the book. It had been pushed into the exact page that I was looking for. I stared at the curly decorative heading that took up half of the yellowing page. The word *Varulv* melted down until it turned into a sinister sketch of a truly fearsome-looking wolf, all fur and bared fangs, dripping blood.

The sheet of paper had been folded in half and stuck into this entry. I picked it up and something fell out. It landed on the table in front of me and I stared at it for a second, frozen to the spot.

It was another Polaroid selfie.

This time Erik wasn't wearing his sunglasses. He was really close to the camera, so close that I could see how bright the blue of his eyes was. The reason he wasn't wearing his sunglasses became obvious as soon as I looked at what was behind him. It had been taken inside the house. It looked like he was standing in a bedroom – his own, I assumed. The background was quite dark. I could just about make out a bed that looked as if it had been made as many times as I'd made mine, which was never.

I stared at the picture for a long time, trying to work out what Erik was taking a picture of. It just looked like a bit of an untidy bedroom, which I guess could have been unusual for a guy of Erik's age but to me looked pretty normal. Then I realized that what I had thought were smudges on the photograph were actually wisps of something.

It was smoke. There were drifting clouds of smoke rising from the bed. When I'd first looked, I'd assumed that the pile of sheets and blankets at the end of the bed had been left there from when Erik had woken up and pushed them out of his way. They were very dark. Again, at first that hadn't struck me as unusual, I'd just assumed they were black. The thing was, as I looked at the photograph, I realized that they weren't black sheets at all. They were white sheets that had been blackened. By smoke and fire. Because someone had set them alight.

The more I looked, the more I saw. The charred, curled ends of the blanket that trailed on to the floor, the black stripes of smoke that had embedded themselves into the walls. The small but clear drops of water cascading from a pillow, presumably from when Erik had realized what was going on and put the fire out. The sooty black handprints all over the place as he'd tried to pat out the last of the flames.

As I was poring over the photograph, I noticed something else. It was a dull gold frame on the wall, half out of shot. It was a mirror. It was *my* mirror. The mirror on my bedroom wall, I mean.

The bedroom in the photograph was *my* room.

I put the photograph down. Suddenly I didn't want to look at it any more. I picked up the sheet of notepaper instead. Erik's handwriting – and I had to assume it was his, didn't I? – looked like a scrawl, as though he'd been in a rush, or maybe very scared.

*Enough is enough,* it said. *I can't win, so I'm going to go. I've got to get Ols away from this place before the snows come and it's too late. Or before*

That was it. Nothing else. He'd stopped writing mid-sentence. Maybe he'd been interrupted and meant to come back and finish whatever he'd been intending to write but never got around to it. Or maybe...

I didn't know what I meant by thinking that 'maybe'. I stopped myself before I got any further.

Part of me wanted to slam the book shut and run away but instead I forced myself to look at the entry about the varulv.

The more I read, the less I understood. Tomas had either been very, very wrong in his translation of the word or he'd lied to us very, very badly.

Varulv definitely did not mean 'wolf' – at least not in any sense that I'd ever thought about one. Tomas had been right when he'd said it was a local word, though. This is what the encyclopaedia had to say about them:

**Varulv (n.)**
A legendary spirit being specific to the folk traditions of northern Scandinavia.

*According to ancient folklore the varulv is a forest spirit, formed of the fusing between a human and a wolf, creating a creature that, although wolf-like in appearance, is neither true wolf nor true human. This creation occurs when a human is bitten by a varulv, causing the victim to become varulv in turn. The transition from human to varulv is said to result in a removal of human identity through memory loss, which according to certain traditions of the myth can* only be restored when the varulv is called by its human name. If the varulv recalls its name, it can be returned to his or her former human self. If this restoration does not occur, the varulv will remain in its wolf-like state forever, as varulv are said to be immortal. Once the last living person to remember the varulv's former name is deceased, the varulv's fate is sealed forever.

Though most extant depictions of the varulv show them as fearsome creatures, they appear to have originally been considered protectors of the great northern forests. The myth's origins are unclear, but it would seem they pre-date written language. The earliest written myths suggest that members of the community were given to the varulv as a spiritual offering to the trees; this offering would then allow the people dwelling amid those forests to do so successfully. One soul from each generation would be made varulv out of respect for the landscape; a sign of understanding that the human population dwelled there at the sufferance of older forces: the trees themselves. However, more sacrifices of the sort would need to be made in unusual circumstances, namely excessive destruction of the forest by human hands. Examples would include a population boom that required more wood be felled for extra homes or if devastation was caused by a human-set fire. To appease the forests, more *members of the community – often, though not always, children – were sent to become ranks of the forest's protectors as both apology and appeasement. In this way it was believed that a balance was established between the forest and the people who lived within its borders. These sacrifices were made only once the first snows of winter had arrived.*

*It is supposed that the ancient legends of the varulv formed the antecedents of the modern populist fantasy of werewolves.*

*See also:* **Kulning**

I shoved the book off my lap and it crashed to the floor with a heavy thump. I didn't want to look at it, any of it. I sat there, my head buzzing, unable to think. I felt as if there was a black hole opening up inside my head and every time I tried to grasp the meaning of what I'd read, how it related to everything that had happened since we'd got here, how *people go missing all the time*, the thoughts slipped away into the abyss.

The trees grow as impatient as we are.
We pace and they writhe,
in the wind,
in the snow.


*They will make payment,*
roars the forest.
*They must.*

# Chapter Twenty-Three

I squeezed my eyes shut, then pressed my fingers into my eyelids so hard I saw sparks. None of this meant anything. None of it did, did it? It was all a daft folk tale, stuff from a time no one remembered any more, that was all.

Except that those kids I'd heard making that weird singing noise had believed there were ghosts in the forest. Except that I'd *seen* something out there. Except that as soon as the previous owner of this place had started tearing up those old trees, something very weird had started happening to him. Except that something had ripped our equipment to shreds so that we couldn't do the same. Except that I'd been chased by a girl that had fangs when all my dad had seen was a wolf. Except that those trees out there seemed to be *angry*.

Except that *people go missing in this forest all the time*.

I opened my eyes again. The book had stayed on

the page with that horrible picture of the varulv.

*I'm going mad,* I thought to myself. *Honest to God batshit crazy. There has to be another explanation. I just have to find it.*

I left the book where it was – there was no way I was reading any more of that crap, not now, maybe not ever – but I picked up the photograph and the note. Then I left the library and went along the corridor to the study. It was still early and the house was silent but outside I could hear the wind and the trees whipping back and forth like they'd like to tear the world apart. Or maybe only everyone living in it.

The other Polaroids and photographs were still on the desk. I spread them out in two lines – Erik's all together and the black-and-white family pictures underneath. I added the latest photograph of Erik I'd found next to the others and made myself look at it again. It still made me shudder. Then I turned the family photographs over again to look at the notes and dates written on the back. I wondered how Erik had known when they had all gone missing. I figured that maybe he'd phoned the local police station to ask. After all, they'd know, right? Even if the records were really old, they would be there somewhere. Anyway, that's the kind of thing that people remember, isn't it? If a whole bunch of people had gone missing from the same place over several decades, *someone* would remember it. So I figured I'd do the same thing.

I didn't get the chance. I was reaching for the telephone when I heard that sound, the hunting horn or song or whatever the hell it was, closer than ever. It rose and rose, a curling, haunting wail almost like a voice but not quite. I froze, trying not to listen to it but hearing it all the same.

Then: "Ingrid! INGRID! Where are you?"

It was Dad. I heard their bedroom door slam and then the sound of running feet. He kept yelling Mum's name and opening and shutting doors. I ran out of the study and along the corridor to the entrance hall.

The double doors were open. They were both slammed back against the walls, wind and snow roaring into the house, the blizzard forcing its way in.

"Dad!" I yelled. "DAD!"

He came running, leaning over the balcony. His face bleached a sickly shade of white when he saw the doors. "Is she out there? Did she go out?"

"I don't know," I said over the sound of the wind as he ran downstairs and around the hole in the floor.

"We have to find her."

"She can't have gone outside," I said. "Not when it's like this. Maybe she went to the bathroom."

"She's not in the bathroom." Dad's voice grated. He went to the door, throwing one arm up to shield his eyes from the vicious, icy spit of the blizzard. "Come on! Help me!"

Neither of us was wearing a coat but I followed him out. The wind was so strong it almost knocked me off my feet as soon as I stepped through the door. I couldn't breathe. The wind crushed itself against my ribcage, forcing the air out of my lungs. I gasped and felt the frozen rasp of ice burn at my throat. My lips instantly began to freeze.

"DAD!" I screamed. "DAD!"

The dark bulk of him turned and flung out a hand, grabbing my arm. He dragged me forwards, off the steps of the house. We'd only staggered a few paces, but it felt as if we'd stepped into a void. I couldn't even see the house any more. All I could see was the chaos of the storm, whirling around us in violent streaks of white. Dad held on to my arm and shook me. I realized he was trying to make me look at something in the snow at our feet.

Footprints. There were footprints leading away from the house, already disappearing under the fresh snow.

We followed them, holding each other up. I was so cold I couldn't feel my fingers. The storm was tearing at me: at my breath, at my clothes, at my skin. I couldn't hear anything but the fury of the wind, I couldn't see anything but the blowing snow.

Then I saw a shape. It wasn't even really that, it was nothing more than a darker fold in the dark white, an interruption in the whirl and blur all around us. It was a fixed point, right in front of us.

It was Mum.

We almost fell over her. I think she was kneeling in the snow. Dad let go of my arm and grabbed at her, trying to drag her up. I did the same. I think she was shouting but I couldn't tell over the bellow and screech of the wind. Then, for a second, the snow cleared. I looked up and the trees were right there over us, a black mass of writhing, hideous branches. Mum had been kneeling right in front of them. I screamed and my voice was torn away by the blizzard. Then I was pulled backwards as Dad started backtracking, dragging Mum and me with him as he tried to make his way towards the house. We carried Mum along with us, stumbling and stopping and starting. I didn't think we'd find the door. I thought the wind would blow us right into the firs. We'd keep going, snow blind and staggering around under the trees until we vanished and no one would ever even know where we went.

*People go missing in this forest all the time.*

Somehow Dad managed to steer us back to the house. We collapsed through the door into a heap. The blizzard chased us in as we lay there, trying to breathe. Then I saw the blood.

"Dad – Mum's bleeding." My voice was high and panicked as I scrambled to my knees. "Dad!" He was already checking her over. Mum sat up and held out her arms. Across them, cutting through her wrists, were ragged slashes weeping scarlet against her white skin.

"She says he can't find me," she said, her voice dazed. "She says I had to show him how to find me. He'll find me now. It's all right. I'm all right. It's so he can find me. Then he can tell me his name."

*He doesn't know his name,* I thought, my mind fizzing with blind panic. *Dorothea lied to you if she told you he did. Because he's one of them, he has to be. He's one of the missing. He's—*

Dad clamped his hands over her wrists and looked up at me with a look of pure terror on his face.

"Call the air ambulance," he said. "Get them here NOW."

I got up and ran to the hallway phone, grabbing it and holding it to my ear.

There was no dial tone. The line was dead.

Dad and I stared at each other across the hole in the floor.

We were completely cut off.

# Chapter Twenty-Four

I helped Dad get Mum upstairs. She was quiet by then, shivering with cold. Dad was as white as milk. Or snow, I guess.

We got her into bed. The bleeding had stopped – the cuts weren't that deep, really, more like bad scratches. I was stunned by everything that had happened but I was still inside my head enough for it to feel wrong and upside down. This was my *mum*. She looked frail against the white sheets, like the abandoned baby bird we'd rescued together when I was a kid. She had too many bones and I could see them all through her skin. I realized her hair was grey and I wondered when that had happened. It hadn't been that colour when we came here. When I left, I shut their door behind me and stood listening for a moment. Dad was talking to her quietly and although I couldn't hear the words, it didn't matter. He probably didn't know what he was saying himself.

I felt something on my cheek and when I went to wipe it away I found my face was wet. I'd been crying and hadn't even known it. I went downstairs to try the phone line again but there was still no dial tone. I stood there with the receiver at my ear and all I could hear was the scream of the wind outside.

I couldn't help going back to that thing I'd read about the varulv. They were mostly wolves, right? Wolves ate meat. They hunted. And what would draw a wolf to a place?

Blood. The smell of blood. That'd probably do it, right?

As I put the phone down I felt something watching me. I turned, slowly. It was Dorothea. She was standing in the shadows. A demon. A twisted, ugly thing. I hated her more in that moment than I had ever hated anything in my life.

"It was you, wasn't it?" I said. "You said something to Mum that made her do it. Because you think there's some supernatural thing out there that's coming to get us."

Dorothea said nothing, just carried on watching

me with her hideous halfway dead eyes.

"You're insane," I told her. "And when we get out of here I'm going to make sure they chain you to a bed and stick you full of drugs for the rest of your miserable, pointless life."

She still didn't say anything. She just smiled. It wasn't a pleasant expression.

"If you ever go near her again, I'll kill you," I warned her. I meant it, too, with every fibre of my being. And you know what? At that moment she was lucky that I didn't know where Dad kept that gun.

I went back into the study. I didn't really know what else to do, so I figured I'd take another look at those photographs. Sice I wasn't going to be able to ask the police about the disappearances — if that's what they were — I wondered if there was another way to find out. I didn't hold out much hope but not even trying would feel worse.

I sank back into the chair behind the desk and sat there for a few minutes, trying to think past the image of the blood dripping from Mum's wrists. It occurred to me that when I'd first found the photographs, I'd been so caught up in looking at them that I hadn't carried on going through the drawer they had been in. I'd pulled out the red notebook but not bothered looking at what else was in there. So I stacked the photographs into a pile on one side of the desk and dragged out the whole thing.

Most of it was more boring paperwork. Unlike the last time, though, this time I didn't mind. I think I'd probably reached peak weird, to be honest. I would have been perfectly happy to find absolutely nothing in there besides yet more notes about timber yields and invoices.

No such luck.

Right at the bottom of the pile there was another notebook. It was about four times the size of the one containing the photographs and much, much older. The covers were dull brown leather. There was a piece of brittle paper stuck to the front, its edges frayed and curling from age. I think both it and the pages inside had once been white but it was so old that it was now more yellow than anything else. There was writing on the label but it had also faded, probably because it had been written in real ink.

*Storaskogen Plantation*, it said, in hand-lettered writing so curly I could barely make them out.

*Yearly Ledger.* The spine cracked as I opened it.

Inside were lists and lists of names and dates. The earliest one, on the very top line of the first page, was 1840. It was the same style of handwriting as was on the label and it said: *Sundberg, Hillof. Plantation Master.*

Under that came other members of the Sundberg family – a woman who was listed as his wife and five children. Then under that were all their employees: the plantation foreman, the workers, the house staff – they were all written down. Their names scrolled across the paper in the same elaborate style.

I turned over page after page. The handwriting changed as the years went by, and so did the names – or some of them, at least. Others stayed listed year after year, sometimes changing position as their jobs on the plantation altered. The Sundbergs stuck around for a long time, two of the sons taking over once the father had carked it. It was kind of mesmerizing, tracing the history of who had lived here through the names and dates on those pages.

Something happened after 1920, though. There began to be fewer names listed. It seemed that every year, more of the staff had left or been let go. The Sundbergs finally sold up in 1925, when another master whose name was Nelius Andersson took over. The Andersson family didn't stay nearly as long – five years later there was someone else, who only stuck it for two years before selling up. By then the lists of names was a fraction of what it had been when the ledger had been started. I flicked through the next decade without having to turn more than three pages.

Another new owner took over in 1938. His name was Lundr Ek. I noticed his name because right underneath it, two other names had been scrubbed out with a frantic scribble of black ink, so heavily that it was impossible to read what had originally been written there. According to the next line over, these had belonged to his wife and son.

I swallowed. I looked further down the list of names and saw that when the Eks had taken up residence, they had hired some different servants.

One was a housemaid called Dorothea Ásviðr, aged fourteen.

My heart thumped harder. I turned the page. Those same two names were blacked out in the next year, too, and the one after that. They had been struck from the list for the next five years. After

1942, their names hadn't even been written in.

In 1943, Lundr Ek had sold the plantation, even though he'd employed a load more plantation workers by then, as if the business had suddenly taken a better turn. The new owner brought with him a wife and infant daughter. I couldn't tell what the baby's name had been, though, because it had been inked over, like the boy and his mother had been in the years before. It was blacked out all the way up to 1949, when the girl disappeared from the record completely.

I reached for the photographs and turned them over until I found the one I knew I should be looking for.

*Girl, aged about 7. Disappeared from Storaskogen in 1949.*

I looked at the little girl in the picture closely and I knew I'd seen her before. It was the girl in my dream, the same one I'd seen dripping with the elk's blood. The one my father had seen as a wolf.

I looked at the list of names of people who had lived at Storaskogen in 1949. There was Dorothea. She'd been promoted to head housemaid by then.

I felt a kind of electricity fizzing in my veins as

I quickly flicked forwards through the dry pages. There were more names scrubbed out and I compared each one to the notes on the photographs Erik had found. They all matched. I knew that if Erik had seen the photograph in the kitchen, it would have had a similar note written on it, too, for that first scrubbed out name back in 1942, when all this had started.

*Boy, aged around 10. Last mentioned at Storaskogen in 1957. Cannot trace without name.*

*Girl, aged around 12. Name unknown. Went missing in 1979. Dead?*

They were all the disappeared that he had photographs for but they weren't the only ones with their names scrubbed from the ledger. There were others in later years, not only children, either – adults as well.

Dorothea had been at Storaskogen the whole time.

I stared at the photographs, trying to process it all. Underneath them were Erik's Polaroids and I caught a glimpse of his grim face, staring back at me. I was struck by a horrible thought and turned back to the book, flipping right forwards to the most recent entry, looking for his name and for Ols's.

I didn't breathe until I saw their names, clear for anyone to read. *Erik Gran, Plantation Master. Ols Gran, son.* Not scrubbed out. Still there, not disappeared.

I looked at the time on my phone. Somehow the day had vanished. It was early afternoon. I was tired – after all, I'd been awake since about 3 a.m. I hadn't eaten anything, but I wasn't hungry. I dragged myself up from the desk and picked up the ledger along with the photographs. There was no way I was leaving them there now, not after what I'd just found out. I figured I'd go and have a nap, then carry on trying to work out what was going on.

I went up to my room and crawled straight into bed. I took my boots off but that was all. The next thing I knew, I was snapping awake. I didn't feel like I'd been asleep, but the room was pitch black. There was a noise coming from the corridor – something shuffling and murmuring. An occasional moan echoed around in the darkness. I lay there, scared. Then I clearly heard a voice. Two voices, in fact, mixed in with the shuffling and moaning.

"It's all right," said one softly, barely above a whisper. "You need some rest, that's all. It'll all be much better in the morning. Let's get you back to bed again."

"No," said the other, more agitated, frayed at the edges and breaking in the middle. "He's found me. But he won't talk to me. I need to know his name."

It was my parents. The first had been Dad's voice, the second was Mum's.

I panicked. Had Mum tried to go outside again? I jumped out of bed so fast that my head spun. I staggered for a moment. Then I made it to the door and clung to the handle as I opened it. Dad was helping Mum along the passageway back to their room, past the end of the corridor where I was. They disappeared from view and I slipped out of my room and walked to the end of the hallway. She must have been in one of the rooms right at the far end, because there was a door standing open down there. It belonged to one of the locked rooms I hadn't been able to get into the first time I'd looked around. I'd peered through the keyhole and seen yet another bed so I hadn't bothered to go back to it.

Dad had his arm around Mum's shoulders as he guided her away. Her head was bowed, her hair messy as it fell over her face and she was moaning softly, her face twisted as she shuffled forwards. Seeing Mum like that turned me cold. Her bandaged arms looked as if they belonged to some weird, half-wrapped corpse.

"His name," my mum muttered to herself again as they reached their room.

"It's all right," my dad soothed. "You had a nightmare, that's all. Just a nightmare."

I stood there until they were inside. Dad shut the door behind them and the house went back to its silence. Nothing sighed, creaked, moaned or mumbled. I took my phone out of my pocket and looked at it. It was almost midnight, so I'd been asleep a lot longer than I'd intended.

The door to the room Mum had been in was still standing ajar, a thick slice of darkness in the gap. I walked to it slowly, almost not wanting to look but needing to all the same. Someone – Mum, I assumed – had forced open the door. There were splinters of wood on the floor and a gouge where the lock had come away from the frame. I hadn't heard it but maybe the noise was what had woken Dad. I pushed the door back on its hinges and reached in to flick on the light.

It was a child's bedroom. I stood on the threshold, looking in and thinking about what Mum had been saying as Dad led her past my room.

*He needs his name.*

I thought of that ledger I'd found earlier that day, with all those scrubbed out names. Had the kid who had slept in this room been one of them? Was he one of the boys in the photographs?

I felt as though the house was holding its breath around me as I walked into the nursery. It was pretty bare. There was a narrow metal-frame bed pushed up against the wall in one corner, a floor-to-ceiling bookcase against the wall beside the window and a largish wardrobe on the opposite side. A threadbare blue-grey rug lay over the floorboards between the bed and wardrobe. It had probably been made from the same blankets that were also on the neatly made bed. Everything had a grey cast to it. It even smelled grey, with that musty tinge in the air that you get in the rooms of old relatives who don't open the windows. The bed was neat, with sheets and a pillow in a pillowcase that had no creases. The walls were a flat white, with no pictures. The bookcase was also white, stacked with ancient volumes of a children's encyclopaedia. There was nothing else. No picture books, even old ones. No toys.

I felt sad as I looked around. The room was stark enough to make me feel the loneliness that was a constant part of life out here in the middle of nowhere. No wonder Mum had come in here and had a fit. And she was right – there was nothing in here to give any clues. There was nothing personal. Nothing even vaguely kid-like, in fact.

I heard a noise behind me and turned. Dorothea stood in the doorway with her arms crossed, staring at me as if she could make me disappear. Clearly me threatening her hadn't made an impression at all. We stared at each other. There was no way I was going to let her know that she scared me.

"Whose room is this?" I asked.

"Not yours," the old bint said pointedly.

"They're all mine," I said, just as pointedly.

She twisted her mouth into a smirk, which seemed to say that I was wrong and that I was a moron all at once and without much effort. The thing was, I knew she was right. This house wasn't mine. It wasn't my parents' either. It was built on land that must have once been forest and that's what it still belonged to. That was obviously what Dorothea believed. And I was beginning to have an idea of exactly what she'd been willing to do in the past to show her faith in that belief.

"What was his name?" I asked her. "The boy who used to sleep here?"

"What boy?" she asked, still sneering.

"I don't know," I said. "The first one you gave to the forest, maybe. Am I right?"

She looked at me steadily. I could almost believe that she hadn't understood what I'd said. I might have bought that from any other old lady but not this one. She knew exactly what I'd said and what it meant. It just didn't worry her in the slightest.

"Who is he?" I persisted. "What's his name?"

The old woman shrugged and then turned to leave the room.

"There's a girl, too, isn't there?" I said as she got to the door. "I've seen her."

Dorothea paused in the doorway but didn't turn around.

"What were their names?" I asked, before she could cross back into the corridor. "What were their names, Dorothea?"

She didn't answer but she didn't move, either. Then she shrugged and the next minute I was alone in that lonely room.

Something drew me to the window. The curtains were drawn shut, made of another shade of grey, heavy material. I pulled one open slightly and looked out.

There he was. The boy. He was standing in a pool of light from one of the lamps on the wall, staring up at me. His arms were crossed and I realized I could see his bare shoulders. He was wearing even less than the first time I had seen him all those weeks ago, sitting crouched opposite the screaming tree. Now he was dressed in nothing but a vest and a pair of shorts and he was calf-deep in the snow, shivering. The same kid, no doubt about it. Was this his room, I wondered? That would make sense.

Then I thought, *Of course it doesn't make sense. He's not there. He can't be there. You're just imagining it.* I put my hands over my eyes. *Stop it,* I told myself. *You can't go mad. You can't. You can't begin to believe the same things that Dorothea does. It's not real. She only wants you to think it is. This is what she wants.*

I opened my eyes again.

The kid was still there, white skin against white snow.

I couldn't tear my gaze away from that shivering, miserable figure and as I carried on looking, I realized something else. He wasn't alone. There were two others down there as well. They were lingering in the full darkness beneath the firs, moving so slowly that at first they seemed like nothing more than shadow. They flowed towards the house, separating from the trees like oil parting from water until they coalesced into recognisable shapes that stood either side of the first boy. Two girls. The one I'd seen covered in blood from the elk's carcass was there. The other one I only knew from the black-and-white photograph of her family I'd been looking at earlier that same day.

*Girl, aged around 12. Name unknown. Went missing in 1979. Dead?*

I stared down at them and they stared back. Were they really there? They couldn't be, could they? This couldn't be real. It couldn't be. I was just making shapes in my head out of darkness. Whatever was down there, they were nothing but figments that would vanish as soon as I pulled up the window. Right?

It took everything in me not to back away but I had to know. My hands were shaking as I heaved the heavy window up on its sash. I leaned out, the ice in the cold air biting at my face. My heart was pounding.

*Don't be there,* I prayed silently. *Don't be there. Don't be there. Don't be there. You're not there. You're not. You can't be.*

I looked down and the world seemed to tip sideways.

They were there. Three impossible children, dressed too lightly for the winter. I gulped in air cold enough to burn my throat but I couldn't breathe.

I stared down and they stared back. Except they weren't staring at me. Their gazes were fixed on the wall beside me.

Out of the corner of my eye I saw something move. I turned my head. There was another kid clinging to the outside wall, level with the window. He was all bones and sharp angles, from his shoulders to his knees to the way his fingers were gripping at the brick with nails embedded so deeply I couldn't see them. His eyes were black, nothing but pupil. He opened his mouth wide and I saw razor-sharp teeth. Then he snarled, lunging for me, slicing one clawed hand out towards my face. I felt the sharp sting as it scraped across my cheekbone.

I screamed and flung myself back into the room, smashing down hard on my tailbone and scooting backwards on my hands, slipping and sliding on the rug. The curtain flapped in a sudden gust of wind. Beyond the open window I could see the firs writhing their spindly branches. I didn't even stand up, I just scrambled for the door.

*Take them*, hiss the trees.
*The debt must be paid.*

*We cannot go in*, we say,
circling beneath their branches.
*They must come out.*
*They must be lost*
*as we were once lost.*

# Chapter Twenty-Five

I threw myself out into the corridor, screaming. Dad came running out of their bedroom, pulling the door shut behind him.

"What is it?" he shouted as I stumbled towards him.

I grabbed his arm, pulling at his sleeve. "They're here, in the house!" I babbled. "They've got in! They're going to kill us! He's here! He's going to—"

He shook me off and then grasped my shoulders. "What is? And what have you done to your face?"

I reached up and touched my cheekbone. My fingers came away covered in blood.

"The gun," I shouted at Dad, trying to drag him back along the corridor, "where's the gun? They're coming!"

"Calm down," he said again, glancing over my head. I twisted around to look but there was nothing behind us. "Calm down and tell me what happened."

I couldn't. I kept expecting to see the kid and his fiendish mates surging down the hallway towards us in a flurry of teeth and claws. I shook my head. "I went into the room where you found Mum. I opened the window and now – now they've got in. They're in the house. We need the gun, Dad. Please—"

Dad let me go and began to walk along the corridor, back the way I'd run. I grabbed his arm but he shook me off.

"We can't," I said. "Dad, we can't go in there!"

But he didn't stop. He strode towards the room and went straight in. I froze, waiting for him to start screaming but he didn't. There was only silence.

"There's nothing here," said his voice, floating to me from inside. "Come and see. Everything's fine."

It took me a minute to make myself move. But I did. I walked slowly to the door and looked inside. Dad was standing at the open window. Little billows of snow were rippling in, falling to the floor, but otherwise the room was empty. There was the bed, the bookcase, the sad little rug crumpled on the wooden floor where I'd slid on it. I could see the curtains blowing open, feel the cold surging in from outside. But there was nothing else. No murderous half-child. No wolf. Nothing at all but an empty room.

"Come here," Dad said again, nodding to the window.

I tried to get a hold of myself. I walked slowly across the room, right up to the window.

"What do you see?" Dad asked. "Look out there and tell me what you see."

I did as I was told. I looked out, through the whirling flakes of white and down to the drift beneath where we stood. There was nothing there at all. There weren't even any footprints. There was nothing but the snow and the trees, laughing at me.

"See?" Dad said, in a very tired voice. Then he put his hands on my shoulders and turned me round. "Look," he said quietly. "I know this has turned into a nightmare. I know it's scary, being stuck here, and what's happened to Mum. But we have to hold it together. All right? You and me. I need you to hold it together."

"Dad," I said. I knew I couldn't have imagined it all, I couldn't have. "Dad, listen. It happened, I know it did. The scratch, this scratch on my face, that proves it, and—"

"Please," he said. I could hear how exhausted he was. "I have to check on your mother. I have to go to bed. Things will be better in the morning. They usually are. Get some sleep. Please."

He left me there in that empty room. I stood still for a few minutes. My cheek was stinging and I could feel the black hole in my head beginning to swallow me up completely. Everything was whirling around up there, lost and untethered.

*They didn't come inside.*

*They didn't come inside.*

*They're out there. I think they're really out there. I think they're real things. But they didn't come inside.*

This is what was going through my head as I staggered back to my room. My ears were buzzing and I kept on shaking – shock, I guess. I curled up on my side under the heavy duvet and tried to think rationally about everything that had happened. Like there's a way to rationalize the sight of a kid stuck to the outside wall of a house in the middle of nowhere.

They didn't come inside. They couldn't have done. They couldn't have got out of that room without Dad and I seeing them in the hallway.

*They didn't come inside.*

I kept clinging to this little piece of information because right then it was a life raft and I was adrift on a churning sea. The window had been open, there had been nothing to stop that thing from surging straight into the room and tearing me apart with whatever it had instead of nails – but it hadn't. Why?

*Because you're mad,* said a voice in my head. *Because you're imagining it all.*

But my cheek was still stinging. I wasn't imagining that. Was I? That was real enough. And something must have done it…

Something outside.

*They didn't come inside.*

*The varulv belong to the forest…*

*The varulv is a forest spirit…*

*I will never give him his name…*

*He needs his name…*

Fragments of sentences Dorothea and Mum had said combined with what I'd read in that old encyclopaedia entry, dancing round and round in my mind, never settling long enough for me to understand them properly. But one thing stuck. The varulv belong to the forest. That's what they exist to protect. Could it be as simple as that? The varulv couldn't come inside because this wasn't their territory? What had the encyclopaedia said? That they could become human again if they're given their names. But if they weren't, they stayed varulv. They remained the forest. They remained outside. They couldn't come in. That had to be the answer, didn't it?

I didn't sleep for the rest of that night. Everything I'd shoved into my brain over the last twenty-four hours kept spinning around, keeping me awake. I lay there, listening to the roar of the blizzard. This one seemed particularly ferocious. The hours ticked by, slow minute by slow minute. I stared at the thick shadows at the edges of my room, imagining them to be shapes of things other than they were: trees growing towards me through the walls, turning inside into outside, bringing the varulv with them hidden in their branches. I was tired, so tired, but I couldn't sleep.

*They didn't come inside.*

*They can't come inside.*

I decided that night that I wasn't leaving the house again until I could be sure I was leaving it forever. Because that was the secret, wasn't it? We just needed to stay indoors. That was why Dorothea had talked Mum into going out into the blizzard and making her arms bleed. The varulv couldn't get into the house so she had to find a way to make us go outside. And there was no way I was letting the varulv take me or my family.

Yeah, so anyway. In case you hadn't already realized, I went off the deep end that night. Isolation will do that to you. Endless snow will do that to you. Lack of sleep will do that to you. Fear will do that to you.

Next morning, I waited in the corridor until I heard Dad leave their bedroom. I didn't really feel like going down and facing Dorothea alone. I figured there was safety in numbers. The two of us against one old woman – what chance did she have?

"Dad."

He jumped, his hand still on the door handle to their room. He turned round and as he did I registered that there were piles of stuff lying all over the corridor outside their door: chairs, blankets, clothes, even the dresser Mum had put her make-up and toiletries on when they first arrived. There must have been nothing left inside the room except the bed Mum was presumably still asleep in and maybe a rug on the floor. Then I realized that when I'd spoken he'd been in the act of quietly turning the key in the lock on their door. He looked guilty as he slipped it into his pocket.

"I don't want to do it," he said, in answer to a question I hadn't asked. "But I'm scared she'll wander off again or use something in there to hurt herself."

"You can't lock her up," I said. Something lurked on my shoulders, a heavy feeling from the deepest part of me, threatening to drag me down. I swallowed. "Dad, that's just—"

"It's for her own good," he said.

"Dad," I said, feeling sick. "Listen. Last night. I swear, outside—"

He held up a hand to stop me. "Don't," he said. "Please. Whatever you think you saw – don't. I've got your mother to deal with. I don't need anything else on my plate right now, all right?"

"But—"

"I mean it," he said. "Whatever you saw, whatever you *think* you saw – it was just a figment of your imagination. There are four people in this house. We are the only people for miles. You *know* that."

We stared at each other for a full minute. What could I tell him? I knew what I'd seen. I also knew it was utterly crazy.

"All right," I said. "But I'm not going outside again. Not until winter's over. You can yell at me all you want. You can threaten to lock me up, too, if you like. But I'm not going out there. And you shouldn't, either. None of us should."

Dad rubbed a hand over his face, over the straggling black-and-white strands of his beard. "We have to. We'll need wood at the very least."

"We can burn furniture."

"We can't burn the furniture."

"We can. It's not even our stuff anyway, is it? It came with the house. It looks like it's been with the house since even before Erik bought it. Why, Dad? Did you ever stop to ask yourself that? Why was he in such a damn hurry to get out of here that he didn't even take his stuff with him?"

Dad put his hands on his hips. He kept frowning, trying to focus. I figured he was pretty tired. I knew how he felt – I was seeing double myself.

"We can't burn the furniture," he said. "It'll be easier to sell this place if it's fully furnished.

278

Furnishing from scratch would cost a fortune. That's why everything is still here. There's no big mystery. It's the way things work up here, that's all."

A word he'd said buzzed in my ears for a second before I repeated it. "Sell?"

Dad shrugged. His shoulders stayed down when he'd finished the motion, defeated. He might as well have been waving a flag of surrender. "You were right. We should never have come here. We'll go back to Stockholm as soon as we can."

I could have hugged him but of course I didn't. "That's ... that's a good idea," I said instead. I was so relieved that my legs felt weak. "That's a good idea, Dad."

"So we can't burn the furniture. We'll need to go out and get more firewood."

"Fine," I said. "Then we'll bring it all in here. All of it. Today. Every last log that's in the shed. And then we never go out of that door again. Not until we leave this hellhole for good. Deal?"

He stood there staring at me. He wanted to ask why, I could tell. He wanted to ask what the problem was with being outside but he couldn't let himself.

"There are things in the forest, Dad," I told him.

"Erik started cutting it down and they're angry. They want us – and not in a good way."

He shook his head. "Please," he said. "Just—"

"All I want is for us not to go outside," I said. "That's not an insane thing for me to want, is it? There's no reason to go out, is there, not once we've brought the logs in? It's not as if we can do any felling. We won't be having any nice walks in the snow. Anyway, it'll be easier to keep an eye on Mum if we're both in the house all the time. Won't it? We won't have to keep her ... locked up."

Dad turned to glance at their door, a pained look on his face. Then he nodded. "All right," he said. "We'll do it."

# Chapter Twenty-Six

I think it took us two loads before Dorothea realized what we were doing. She fluttered around us like an angry bug as Dad and I hauled log after log out of the sled. We dumped them in an untidy pile beside the fireplace in the front room. We were both beyond caring how the place looked. Besides, we were racing the light. If I had to go outside, I didn't want to have to do it in the pitch black.

"Mess!" Dorothea squawked as we overturned another load of logs on to the polished floor. "What are you doing? Mess!"

"Get out of the way," I told her as we headed out for another load.

"You can't bring more in!" she told us, skittering along beside Dad as far as the front door.

"We'll be bringing in the rest of the wood now, Dorothea," Dad told her matter-of-factly. "It'll be safer for all of us if we don't have to leave the house in the middle of winter."

At that she stopped dead. I saw a look of shock on her face that made me want to smile.

"What's wrong, Dorothea?" I asked innocently as Dad went out ahead of me into the storm. "It's a good idea, isn't it? Not to go out? I mean – winters are so hard up here. And … people go missing in the forest all the time. Right?"

She narrowed her eyes, the tip of her tongue flicking out to wet her dry lips. She fixed me with her eyes.

"You think you're so clever," she whispered. "But you won't outwit the forest. No one ever does. It will take what it is owed."

At that moment I knew I'd been right. We'd be safe as long as we didn't leave the house. The varulv couldn't come inside unless she gave them their human names but that would mean taking them away from the forest. Then they'd just be children – forgotten, out of time and useless.

"What are their names, Dorothea?" I whispered back. "Tell me their names."

Her lips curled back. I half expected to see fangs but instead there were only two lines of old, yellow teeth. "Never," she hissed. "They will never know their names."

I left her there and staggered out into the snow after Dad. The blizzard hit me full in the face but I was so used to it by now that I didn't even really pay it attention. I felt light-headed, as though I were dreaming, except with this weird electric charge skating across the surface of my skin. How could any of this be real?

But it didn't matter. It didn't even matter if we'd all gone as crazy as Dorothea. All we had to do was stay inside the house and wait until the phone line was back up. Then we could be evacuated. We'd get out of here and go back to Stockholm, get Mum well again and forget that any of this had ever happened.

I stumbled and slid after Dad, wiping snow out of my eyes and trying to focus on the shed in front of us rather than the black, twisting wall of trees to my right. I'd just reached the door when I heard something over the roar of the wind. It soared into the air, rising and falling like notes from an instrument I didn't recognize. It was that haunting, lilting song again. It scythed right through the snow-clogged air and out into the forest, piercing the darkness. The indistinct shape of Dorothea was standing in the light from the open doorway. She seemed to have her hands cupped around her mouth but as I watched she dropped them to her sides. The weird music blew away with another gust of icy wind. Maybe I'd never really heard it in the first place.

"Come on," Dad shouted to me impatiently. "You're the one who wants to get this done today."

They cannot hide from the trees.
The forest does not forgive.
The debt will be paid.
They will belong to the trees,
as we belong to the trees.

We are the storm.
We circle.
We wait.

# Chapter Twenty-Seven

Over the next few days more and more snow piled against the house, as if it were trying to bury us alive. Dad constantly tested the phone line but it stayed down. Dorothea kept trying to get me to go outside.

"The water pipes will freeze," she'd say. "You need to go out and cover them up." Or, "There are food stores in the outbuildings that I need. I can't carry them on my own. You'll have to get them for me. Take the sled."

I always refused. Well, actually, I always answered her with a question. "What are their names, Dorothea?" I'd ask. "Tell me all their names. Do that and I'll go outside for you."

She wouldn't, so we were at a standoff. She probably would have badgered Dad to do it but he spent every minute he could with Mum. He was losing weight, like she was. His beard grew longer every day.

Outside, blizzard after blizzard raged. The storms had become worse once we'd stopped going out. Perhaps the weather was as furious with us as Dorothea. *Perhaps they're one thing,* I thought as I lay awake listening to the wind heave itself against my windows like a battering ram. *Perhaps Dorothea's the outside, inside. Sent to make us pay for thinking we could ever own this place.*

I tried to talk Dad into locking her up. "She's not safe, Dad. It was her who talked Mum into going out in the snow to cut herself. And she keeps trying to get me to go outside."

Dad shook his head. "I know she's unpleasant and odd," he said, "but she's just old and set in her ways."

I knew it was more than that but every time I tried to explain he shut me down. And I got why. I did.

I dug out Erik's Polaroids and the ledger from where I'd hidden them under my mattress. I hadn't looked at them for a while. There hadn't been much point. But now I laid the photos out in a line on my bed and realized that they made more sense. The jack-knifed truck that had stranded him so that he'd had to walk a long way back to the house, the fallen tree on the car that had forced him to do the same, even the fire in the woodshed. They were all about making sure he had to be outside in the forest for a prolonged period of time so that the varulv could find him.

I wondered where his kid – Ols – had been for all of these incidents. There was no sign of him in any of them. Unless Dad had told me, I wouldn't even have known that Erik had a son. I wondered if maybe Erik had done the same as Dad had with Mum – locked him in a room in the house and made sure only he had the key.

That idea made me pretty uncomfortable but it also made me think about the door to my room. It had a keyhole, the same as the rest of them, but I'd never had the key. I wondered whether Dad or Mum had it, or at least knew where it was. Right then I quite liked the idea of being able to lock myself in. At least then Dorothea wouldn't be able to get to me.

That night was one of those times when I didn't know I was almost asleep until I woke up. One minute I was looking at the photographs and thinking about what tactics Dorothea might use to get us to leave the house, the next I was opening my eyes. I'd obviously squirmed around to get comfortable, because I had rolled over the photographs. They were scattered everywhere. The ledger was wedged under my hip. I sat up, blearily rubbing my eyes.

Then I smelled smoke. For a second I thought I was imagining it – that I'd been dreaming about fire before I woke up and now my brain was registering smoke when it wasn't really there. But then I heard a sharp crackle from the corner of the room.

I wasn't dreaming.

There was a fire.

Right then.

Right there.

*In. My. Room.*

I leaped up. Dark grey smoke was rising from one corner, billowing to the ceiling and then rolling along it in a thick wave that spilled towards my bed. The flames were reaching after the smoke, flickering and dancing up the walls, growing bigger and bolder by the second. I could hear the snap and crack as they licked at the ancient wallpaper, eating it bit by bit. Before I could think, the flames were as high as my knee and then as high as my chin and then—

I must have screamed. I must have done, though I can't remember making the sound. The heat was a blanket over my face – suffocating, blinding. My eyes watered and everything was blurred. I ran for the door as the room dissolved in flame and fury, the hiss and fizzle of the fire snapping at my heels. My fingers were gripping the handle when something – some voice that must have been my subconscious – yelled at me. I stopped.

*This is what she wants. This is a way to get you all out of the house.*

I swung around to face the flames, then spotted the glass of water on the little table beside my bed. I lunged for it – two steps across the room – and flung it at the fire, glass and all. I might have well have spat for all the good it did. The flames didn't even splutter.

I know I was shouting by this point, because in some weird, detached way I could hear myself, as if from very far away. I ran to the window, wrenching it up on its sash. The cold air rushed in, fanning the flames so that they stretched and heaved. I grabbed the top blanket from my bed and started scooping armfuls of snow on to it. Outside, the firs stood watching, black and silent.

I heaved the blanket towards the fire, sopping wet with melting snow. As I dragged it the door to my room flew open and Dad stood there, one arm up around his face to protect it from the smoke. He was yelling but it wasn't until later that my brain registered what he was saying. I threw the sodden blanket over the flames. There was a hissing sound, hot steam billowing into my face. Something bit at my fingers. I looked down to see a bright orange flame eating at my skin. It was scorching a line across my knuckle, the skin bubbling and blistering. I stumbled backwards. Dad was still yelling.

It sounds weird but I didn't feel any pain. I think I was too hopped up on adrenaline and fear. I lunged for the bed again and dragged the duvet to the window, gathering as much snow as I could, the ice sizzling against my burned skin. Then I felt hands on my arms. They dragged me backwards, making me stop.

"We have to get out of here!" Dad screamed in my ear.

"No!" I wrenched myself out of his grip and dragged up the duvet. I threw it over the faltering fire, then dropped to my hands and knees and patted desperately at the last of the flames. The smoke roiled up against the ceiling, pooling there as the fire died. I could hear Dad breathing hard. I was, too. I dropped my head on my one good hand and gasped for air. The smell of burning hung around us but the heat was rapidly being replaced with freezing gusts from the still-open window.

Dad dragged me backwards. We both collapsed in a heap against the bed. He grabbed my hand and looked at it, a horrified expression on his face. I looked properly, too. There was a red slash across it and bits of my skin were hanging off but I couldn't feel anything. I was numb. Dad hurried to the window and grabbed handfuls of snow. He came back and packed it onto the burn.

"What happened?" he asked.

I shook my head, dazed. "There was – a fire."

"How did it start?"

"I don't know."

"Were you smoking up here? Have you got cigarettes?"

We looked at each other. When I was little, I used to ride on his shoulders. He'd pretend to be an elephant, harrumphing about, putting his head down and lifting his shoulder to his nose so that his arm made a trunk. He'd reach up with it and

292

feed me sweets over his shoulder, or try to tickle me under the arms.

Suddenly I wanted to go back there. I burst into tears.

Dad seemed a bit confused by my crying. To be honest, it was a bit of a surprise to me, too. I don't spend a lot of time showing people my softer side. I don't *have* a softer side. Really.

"It's all right," he said. "It's all right, you're all right. Look," he said, pulling me up so I was sitting on the edge of the bed. Then he went to the window and scooped up more snow to put on my burn. "Tell me what happened. I'm listening."

"I keep telling you," I said, between breaths. "It's Dorothea."

"It can't have been Dorothea," he said.

"Who else could it have been?" I shouted.

Dad held up a hand. "Calm down."

"Calm down? Did you see what just happened?"

"It was an accident," he said. "You must have fallen asleep with one of your candles still burning and knocked it over." He looked round, then saw something on the floor and went over to pick it up. He held it up for me to see. It was the end of a stubby little candle. "See?"

Crying was suddenly the last thing in my mind. I could have punched him. Why was he always such an idiot? Why couldn't he *see*? "It wasn't a candle, Dad. I didn't even have a candle burning. I didn't do this. Anyway, how could that candle, over there—" I pointed to where he'd found it, below the mirror hanging on the wall, "have started that fire on the other side of the room?"

Dad frowned. I could see he got my point. "There's no other explanation."

"There is! I keep telling you that. It was Dorothea. She's dangerous, Dad."

"Why on earth would Dorothea set fire to her own home? Eh?" Dad's voice was as exasperated as mine. "Explain that. She'd be in danger herself. Not to mention that she'd be homeless."

"She wouldn't have let it get that far. She only wants to make us go outside. She was trying to force us – me – to go outside. She's done it before! Look—" I scrabbled around with my one good hand trying to find the Polaroid of this room when it had been Erik's but I couldn't. It wasn't on the bed, or on the floor beside it. "She's taken it!" I said, and I admit, I probably sounded like a bit of a nutter by this point. "It's gone! It was here when I fell asleep!"

Dad grabbed me and forced me to be still. "Stop it," he said. "Look – this has all been a shock, I understand that. It was an incredible thing you did, putting out that fire. But I want you to promise me that if anything like this ever happens again, you won't try to stop it. You'll flat out run. OK? Because nothing out there is going to hurt you and nothing in here is worth your life. Do you understand?"

I stared at him. He'd sounded more Dad-like with that speech than he had for years. It reminded me again of how when I was little and I'd just assumed that he knew everything. When had that ended? Like riding on his shoulders. When was the last time I'd done that? Because there had been one final time, even if neither of us had known it when it happened. Last things must happen all the time and we don't even notice until it's too late. Like cutting down the last gnarled tree in a forest that has been in the same place for as long as there have been forests. It just happens and we move on. We replace that last thing with other things and we forget that something else once existed. We forget that it was important, or maybe we just never knew. But those things, once they've gone, we can't ever get them back again. And one day one of those things will be the most important thing there ever was and we won't know it until it's too late.

But what if we did know? What would we be willing to do to keep those things forever?

Dad broke the silence by patting my shoulder. "Come on," he said. "Let's get you into another bedroom and I'll sort out that hand. We'll leave all this mess until tomorrow."

"I want to be near you and Mum," I said. "Please."

He smiled. "Sure. I think we can manage that."

# Chapter Twenty-Eight

Before we found me a new bedroom, Dad wanted to try the phone line again. The fact that he'd tried it about fifteen times throughout the previous day and it had always been dead didn't seem to put him off.

"You never know," he said. "And anyway – listen. The storm's died down. So if the line's going to be up again any time, it'll be now, won't it?"

I was kind of smiling as I followed him down the hallway to the nearest phone. Say whatever you like about Dad, he's forever optimistic. Maybe that's all his stubborn streak is, really. He wants to believe that the best thing he can imagine could be the truth. I guess I can get behind that.

Anyway, for once he turned out to be right.

"There's a dial tone!" he shouted, even though I was standing right next to him.

"Call the police!" I said, my heart thumping. "Tell them to get us out of here!"

Dad was already dialling. I could see his hand gripping the receiver so hard that his knuckles turned white. I held my breath as I watched his face. It lit up as soon as the call was answered.

"Yes," he said, "yes – hello. This is Martin Stromberg, at the Storaskogen plantation, Norrbotten. I called a few weeks ago about a crime that had been committed… No! No – don't transfer me, that's not— We need to be evacuated. We're snowed in with not enough provisions. There's been a house fire and my wife is ill… Yes. Yes."

There was a pause. I realized I had my hand on Dad's arm, gripping his sleeve. His face changed a little. I held my breath again.

"OK," he said. "How long do you think…? OK. That's great. Thank you. We'll be waiting."

He put the phone down.

"They are coming, right?" I said, feeling slightly panicked at the look on his face. "They are going to evacuate us, right?"

He nodded and patted me on the shoulder again with a faint smile. "They are. But there's another blizzard rolling in. They can't fly in it. We'll have to wait until it's cleared. They think perhaps another two or three days, that's all."

I sagged, feeling like a puppet that had had my strings cut. "Three *days*?"

"It's fine," Dad told me, back to his usual peppy self. "That's not long, is it?"

"All right," I said. "I guess we'll be OK as long as we stay indoors."

Dad sighed, but he was still smiling. "Yes. We'll stay indoors. Now, come on – let's find a first aid kit and a new bedroom for you. I'm worried about that hand."

We decided on the room right next to theirs. It was small and didn't have much furniture but I was fine with it. Dad pulled some extra blankets out of a cupboard in the corner and I watched as he spread them over the bed. Then I sat down and he opened the first aid kit and found some burn cream and a bandage. My hand didn't feel that bad, to be honest. I think it looked worse than it was. But it was nice to have Dad worried about me. In some strange way it felt as though we were starting over. In three days – maybe less – we'd be out of here. They'd brought me up here to start a new life but maybe it would turn out that going back to our old one would be where we really started over.

"Dad." I took a deep breath and hesitated but I knew if I didn't ask now there might not be another time that felt right. "About Mum. This … her being ill … it started before we came here, didn't it? It wasn't this bad. But there was something, wasn't there? What happened?"

Dad sighed. He paused for a moment, then finished fastening the bandage and sat down next to me on the bed. "We would have told you," he said, "but the time never seemed right."

I felt sick. "Told me what?"

"We were going to have another baby," he said, clasping his hands together. "We had you when we were very young. We thought it was the right time to add to the family – before we got too old to raise another child. But Mum had a miscarriage earlier this year. The doctors don't think she'll be able to have another baby now."

This wasn't what I'd been expecting to hear by any stretch of the imagination. I blinked, shocked to feel tears in my eyes. My ears buzzed.

"We were both devastated but your mum – she blamed herself. She thought it was because she'd

300

been working too much. I kept telling her that was ridiculous – that of course it wasn't her fault and no one could have done anything about it. But that didn't help. She talked to someone – professionally, I mean – but they wanted to give her anti-depressants and you know what she's like about drugs."

I did. She didn't even really like taking painkillers.

Dad tangled his fingers together. "She decided that a change was what she needed. She found this place online and fell in love with the idea of coming up here. I wasn't keen – I wasn't sure it would be a good idea to move so far away from everything that was familiar but it was the happiest I'd seen her for ages, so I thought, well, we should give it a try. I figured there'd be a way to make it work."

I nodded. Yeah, that sounded like Dad.

"I should have known," he said. "I should have known the isolation would be bad, not good."

"It's not your fault," I said. "She was OK to begin with, wasn't she? It was that accident with Alisa…"

"She blamed herself for that, too. As if she was suddenly responsible for every one of those kids." Dad frowned. "But this boy she keeps talking about now. She talked about him even before the

301

accident. She told me she'd seen him up in the attic, but Dorothea had told her she'd been imagining it. She was scared Dorothea was right and that she was seeing things."

"I was there when Mum told Dorothea that," I said. "Dorothea was really evil about it." I frowned, thinking. Was it possible that Mum had really seen something up there? But I was sure the varulv couldn't get inside.

"Anyway," Dad said, with a sigh. "This move was a disaster in every sense, as I believe you said it would be before we even left Stockholm."

"I'm sorry, Dad," I said. "Maybe if I'd been less of a brat – maybe if I'd paid more attention to Mum—"

He rested a hand on my shoulder. "Don't. That way madness lies. 'What if's are no good to anyone. What matters is what we do next. So we'll go back to Stockholm, the three of us, and you and I will do whatever it takes to help your Mum get better. All right?"

I smiled. "Yeah. All right."

Dad stood up. "Try to get some sleep. We're right next door if you need us."

We said goodnight. I sat there for a while after

he'd left, realizing how selfish I'd been for too long. Well, all that was going to change, I told myself. In three days, whatever happened, we'd be out of here and on our way back to Stockholm. And I'd begin to be a better person.

I was about to get into my new bed when I remembered the photographs and the ledger. They were still in my old room and it suddenly seemed to me that I shouldn't leave them there. They were evidence, after all. Of what, I wasn't entirely sure but they were all I had to prove that Dorothea had done terrible things in the past and would be capable of doing more, given half a chance.

I didn't want Dorothea getting hold of them, so I went back to get them. By now the adrenaline had leeched out of me, leaving me bone-tired. But at least I wasn't scared any more. The police were coming for us. Nothing could happen to us now without them knowing about it, so surely not even Dorothea would be insane enough to try anything. *We're safe*, I thought. *As long as we stay inside the house for the next three days, we're safe.*

I quickly gathered up the photos from where they'd been scattered over the floor, including the one of the fire that I thought had disappeared. Actually, it had wafted down to the floor and under the bed. I stuck them in the front of the ledger and then picked up my phone, too. I tried not to look at the great black patch of ash that had scorched the wall. The room still smelled of burning, an acrid, clogging taste in the air that got into my nose and worked its way into my throat. As I turned round I caught a glimpse of myself in the old mottled mirror and stopped. The angle of my reflection was wrong. It was tilting in a different direction than usual.

I stepped closer to the mirror. There was a gap down its right-hand side, barely big enough to fit my fingers into. I'd assumed it was fixed flat to the wall, but now one side of it had been pushed outwards. Then I realized why. It wasn't a mirror at all. It was a door. There were hinges on the other side of it, set so close to the wall that you'd only notice them if you looked closely, which I never had.

I pushed my fingers into the gap and pulled. The mirror-door swung open silently, revealing a narrow passageway leading away into pitch black.

Servants' passageways. They must have been all over the house, running between rooms and behind hallways. It explained how Dorothea managed to disappear in one place and reappear in another. I wondered where she was right now – maybe even lurking back there somewhere in the dark, watching me with those narrow, watery eyes. The thought sent a chill down my spine and I shut the door quickly, closing out the darkness. At least I knew how she'd got in here to set the fire. She must have dropped the candle she'd used as she scrambled back into the darkness. Maybe I'd woken up and startled her. Either way, I'd show my discovery to Dad in the morning – it might convince him that I'd been right about Dorothea. We'd go down that corridor together – not only this one, but all of them. We'd uncover every secret corner and hideaway she had.

I tried to remember if there could be anything hiding a door like this in Mum and Dad's room. I didn't think there was. Dad had dragged out most of the furniture – he definitely wouldn't have left a mirror in there. So they were probably safe for now. But I decided that I wasn't going to sleep. I was going to stand watch outside their door, in case. (This was all part of the 'me being a better person from now on' plan.)

As I was coming out of my old room, I heard something. A soft creeping, the very smallest hint of a step, like a large spider walking across a piece of paper. The sound was coming closer, inching its way towards me. I thought it was Dorothea. It was the same kind of movement as her footsteps, that weird scuttle. I stuck my phone in my pocket and squashed myself against the wall. A tight, anxious feeling knotted itself into my stomach. A faint light bobbed towards me, thin and flickering. It glanced off the walls, showing up the uneven shabbiness of the wallpaper in a way I'd never noticed before. It made me think of the house as a huge coffin, with all of us inside mouldering away in the endless dark.

The scuttle got closer and closer, flickering in and out of my hearing.

The light reached the end of the hallway.

It wasn't Dorothea.

The yellow glow cast by the candle revealed a small boy. I froze, not even breathing, but he didn't look in my direction. He walked past the end of the corridor from the direction of my parents' room, looking straight ahead. He was barefoot, walking carefully on his tiptoes, deliberately trying not to make a noise. He'd almost perfected it, but not quite.

My heart thumped painfully. He couldn't be a varulv. So what was he? A ghost? But since when did ghosts need candles to see by? Since when did ghosts have to work hard to move silently?

*Occam's Razor,* I heard my dad say. It was one of his favourite sayings. *The simplest explanation is usually the truth.*

If this kid wasn't a varulv and wasn't a ghost, then what else could he be?

When he'd passed out of view, I put the ledger down on one of the little tables in the hallway and I coasted along to the end of the corridor in my socks. There's a tip for you, right there – if you want to move around silently on a polished wooden floor, don't go barefoot and don't walk. Wear socks and slide, like you're pushing off on a skateboard. See? I do know some things. Go me.

The kid wasn't in the corridor any more but I could still see the faint yellow light of his candle. He'd gone into the room Mum had broken into on the night I'd seen the varulv out of the window. I stood at the end of the corridor, waiting to see if the boy would come back out again but he didn't. The candle glow hung there, faint and persistent. I wondered what he could be doing – there wasn't anything in there. Was he sitting on the floor reading the encyclopaedias or something? Then, suddenly, the light disappeared. It plunged me into absolute darkness.

I fumbled to turn my phone on. The faint yellow glow was replaced by a faint blue one.

*Screw this,* I thought. I walked down the corridor and into the room.

The kid had vanished. I stuck my head out of the door and looked back down the corridor in both directions but I already knew there was no way he could have come back out of the room again without me seeing.

I stood there thinking. The house was silent.

Except that it wasn't.

I could hear footsteps. They were really, really faint, but once I'd heard them, that's definitely what they were. I went to the door again and looked down the corridor but there was no sign of anyone. I went back into the room, stepped right up to the wall beside the little bed and put my ear against it. I could hear the footsteps through it, still there but growing fainter.

I checked behind the empty bookcase and the wardrobe. I kicked the rug aside, in case there was a hatch in the floor, but no – nothing. I stopped. Where else was there to look? The bed? But that only reached a metre up the wall and there was no sign of a door behind it.

I kneeled and peered underneath it anyway. What's that Sherlock Holmes quote that Dad loves so much? *Once you eliminate the possible, whatever remains, no matter how improbable, must be the truth.* And there it was. A tiny hatch set in the wall. If you wriggled under the bed it would be possible to open it and slip through, but I wasn't too keen on that idea, so I got back to my feet and tugged the bedframe away from the wall instead.

I kneeled down and pulled at the hatch. The door swung open silently, but easily enough – it had obviously been used recently.

The only way to get through it was head first on my hands and knees. I shuffled forwards, holding my phone out in front of me as a light, bumping my head and scraping my shoulders as I pushed myself through the narrow gap. Thankfully, as soon as I was through the wall, I could stand up properly. The first thing I saw once I was back on my feet was that there were steps immediately in front of me, leading down.

I thought about going back and getting Dad out of bed but decided against it. I was afraid but I figured that even I could handle one little kid on my own. After all, I wasn't dealing with some weird evil spirit, was it? Knowing that made me feel kind in control in a way I hadn't been since we got to Storaskogen, I guess. So I carried on. I headed down the stairs as if everything was completely normal.

I know, I know. How stupid am I?

The kid was at the bottom of the stairs. He was on his knees in what seemed to be a mountain of old blankets. He'd piled them all up on top of one another, unevenly, like an over-sized bird's nest. He was kneeling right in the middle of it, having stood the candle on top of an old wooden box that was next to the pile. The kid was staring up at me with scared eyes so huge that they seemed to be taking over most of his face.

I stopped for a couple of seconds, hovering on the

second-to-last step. I didn't really know what to do but there were two things I was completely certain about. One, the boy seemed to have been living inside the walls of this house for a while and two, I felt sorry for him. Really, properly, desperately sorry, because whoever he was and whatever he was doing here, it looked as though he'd had a pretty miserable time of it.

I put my phone in my pocket and took a couple of steps forwards into the corridor. There was a narrow door to my right, which, if I'd been smarter, I would have kept an eye on as I passed.

"Hey," I said, my voice sounding weird in the silence. "Look, there's nothing to be scared of. I only wanted to say hi. OK?"

He looked past me, a fresh terror flickering behind his eyes. I felt a cold breeze waft from behind us and as I turned, something came towards me, whistling through the air. Whatever it was turned out to be pretty solid. I know that because the second it smashed into my skull, it knocked me out cold.

The forest watches.
We see.

*We must have them all,*
roar the trees.
*There is a debt.*
*It must be paid in full.*
*It must be paid now.*

# Chapter Twenty-Nine

I've got no idea how long I was out for. I came around a bit at a time, in flashes of hurt and darkness and a cold that seemed to reach deeper than my bones.

The smell got to me even before consciousness did – a suffocating, brutal stench that shoved its way up my nostrils and into my mouth. It was thick and horribly real. I opened my eyes but there was no light. None at all. I don't mean that all I had to do was let my eyes adjust until they could deal with how little light there was. I mean I was in complete and utter darkness.

Have you got any idea what that's like? It's pretty rare. Even in the middle of the night, it's not completely dark. There are stars, for example. They won't light your way but they're something you can *see*. To really experience total darkness, you have to lock yourself in a cellar that has no windows or lights and make sure you don't have a torch or a phone. Trust me – it's terrifying.

I came around upright, although I wasn't quite standing. My head was lolling on my left shoulder and that shoulder was leaning against something hard. In fact, it was like I'd been wedged into the corner of a cupboard. A damp, cold cupboard that reeked of snails but much, much worse.

I lifted my head. Lights swam in my vision, sparking with electric rainbow colours. I could taste blood in my mouth, and the rest of me was bruised and battered.

Panic set in when I tried to move my arms and couldn't. I realized that my hands had been tied together at the wrists. I pulled at them, trying to wrench them apart. But the rope was thin and strong, and all I managed to do was make my wrists raw and the burn on my hand hurt like crazy. I shouted, my voice rasping through a sore, dry throat. But it was as if I was shouting while someone held a pillow over my face – the sound fell dead as soon as it left my mouth. I tried to turn round, but my feet were on something sharp and uneven that made me think I'd fall off a precipice if I stepped the wrong way. Whatever was underfoot was slippery, too, and slid and squelched slightly as I moved. Whatever it was gave off waft after waft of rotting, noxious fumes. I gagged and tried to swallow back the vomit.

*Stop panicking,* I told myself. *Calm down. Count to ten. Stop panicking!*

It didn't really work. I never was very good at doing as I was told, even when I was the one doing the telling. I carried on wrenching and shuffling and shouting until my voice was hoarse. Then a last jerk of my hands made me stumble. I fell forwards and smashed my head against what was right in front of me, which happened to be another wall.

I must have blacked out again.

The next time I came round I jumped awake as if someone had shaken me. I had slumped to my knees, but the space I was in was so narrow that the walls had stopped me from reaching the floor, so I was still mostly upright. My throat was still sore from all the shouting I'd done the first time round, which told me I hadn't been out very long. I struggled upright and tried to get my panic under control before it could grip me. I did that by trying to assess my situation.

*Trapped.*

*Head wound.*

*No light.*

*Hands tied.*

*Cold.*

All in all, that didn't really help with the panicking.

At first I didn't think I'd be able to do anything about any of those things and then I remembered my phone. I'd shoved it into my pocket when I'd started to speak to the boy. If my hands had been bound behind my back, I would have been completely screwed but they weren't – they were tied in front of me, which gave me a spark of hope. I reached for the pocket, praying that the phone was still there. It was – I could feel its outline.

I tried to untangle my fingers enough to edge the phone out. It was a tricky business, not least because I couldn't stop shaking and the pain from my burn was horrible. Still, I managed to shuffle the phone centimetre by centimetre until I'd almost got the whole thing out...

...and then I lost my grip.

I swore and grabbed for it but I was too slow. I felt it bounce off my knee and thought I'd lost it forever but then it hit my calf and hung there.

My headphones! They'd been wrapped around it and had caught inside the pocket. I snatched at the phone and angled the jack out of the socket. I worked out which way round it was and thumbed the 'On' button, managing to type in the pin even though I was still shaking like a leaf.

No signal. Of course.

I swallowed hard. At least I had a bit of light. That was a start. Maybe I'd be able to see a way out of wherever I'd ended up. I held it away from me, blinking until the afterimage of the screen had lessened. Then I looked around.

The first thing I saw was white. Well, I say it was white – it was mostly white, although in places it had clods of something grey clinging to it, along with tangled, wispy strands of what my aching brain thought was wool.

It wasn't wool. It was hair. I was standing beside a skeleton, my chin level with the top of the skull.

And that's how I found out what had happened to Erik.

I started screaming.

I'll be honest, the screaming carried on for quite a long time. Not that it did me any good. The

318

sound just hung there right in front of me. I must have blacked out again, because I don't remember stopping. I came round again with my head against the left wall. I'd slumped as far to my knees as the small space would allow, which thankfully wasn't that far, or I'd have been crouching in Erik.

The second I remembered what else was in that place with me, I felt the panic surging up through me like a tide. It's a real thing, panic – as real as a car coming right at you through a red light. If it hits you, it smashes you into a million pieces. I tried to keep my nerve. I did that by turning round until I faced the other wall and couldn't see his rotting corpse. Then I flicked on the phone again.

Wherever I was, it was narrow. The wall I was staring at – and it was stone, not wood – was barely wider than my shoulders. If I'd been able to lift both hands independently, I wouldn't even have to unbend my elbows to touch the walls. Through the fog in my mind, I figured the wall in front of me was probably a metre wide, and from what I'd briefly seen before I'd lost it, that seemed to be the case for the other three adjoining it, too.

I lifted the phone and looked up into the dim

light. The walls stretched away above my head. It was a small tunnel, I realized, and for a second I wondered if I was so disoriented that I'd thought I was standing when really I was lying on my side. I tried to crawl forwards and then felt stupid, because gravity told me very definitely that I'd got it right the first time. I also realized that the 'tunnel' wasn't straight. It was at a slight angle. Right at the top, which was at least five metres away, there seemed to be a hatch.

A chute. I was in some kind of chute. That was good, right? I mean, chutes go from one place and end up in another. So that meant there had to be another way out of here.

The problem was, that meant I had to look around. Like, properly. Not only at the side of the stone prison right in front of me. I had to look at what was behind me and below me as well. Which meant I had to look at the corpse. I had to look at Erik.

I leaned my forehead against the wall. *Come on,* I told myself. *He's dead, that's all. Do it. Just do it.*

It took me a while to talk myself into it. I turned the phone off and stood there in the silent dark for a while, trying to pretend that there was absolutely nothing mental about this situation in the slightest. I was going to get myself together and then start rooting about in the decaying remains of a murder victim to get myself out of a predicament that would otherwise mean I was a serial killer's next hit. Absolutely nothing to see here, move along home, folks, move along home.

*Home.* I thought of our house in Stockholm, about my life there and how boring it had been, and right then I wanted nothing more in the universe than to be going to school every day, doing the same things day in, day out.

*If I get out of here,* I promised myself, *I'm never putting a foot wrong again. Ever.*

Yeah, yeah, I know. Famous last words. But let's not go there, OK?

I flicked the light of my phone back on, steeled myself, and turned round.

Erik stared back at me in all his hideous deadness. Dorothea's *modus operandi* was visible in the huge dent in his skull, from which a spider's web of feathery cracks spun out across the dome of yellow-white bone. There were still gluts of skin clinging to his head and wisps of blond hair, longer than in the photos I'd seen.

Erik's clothes were hanging off him in tatters. I'd never thought of him as a short person, but even though we were standing opposite each other, he only came up to my chin. Then I looked down and realized why. He was kind of slumped at the knees. His feet and ankles were hidden under a heap of rocks that seemed to have been piled up around him. The rocks were mired in a miasma of sludge.

The sludge was also Erik.

I think I probably screamed a bit more for a while, then. It wasn't so much the sludge – although I'm not saying that wasn't a pretty major factor – but the rocks. The rocks meant that whatever was at the bottom of the chute was completely blocked off. Even if my hands weren't tied together and even if I could deal with sticking them into the Eriky soup, where would I put them? There was hardly room to move. There definitely wasn't any room to pile anything in a corner out of the way.

Once the latest bulldozer of panic had smashed me square in the chest and rolled away again, I looked up at the hatch overhead.

I tried to climb. Imagine that for a moment: me trying to get out of that place. Five metres doesn't sound like a lot really, does it? Well, it could have been one metre and it still would have been impossible. Or it was for me, anyway. No matter what I did, I couldn't free my hands, so I was pretty much climbing one-handed. Except that it was worse than that, because my hands were tied palms together, so I couldn't find a way of gripping with even one of them. In the end, I tried to copy a move I'd seen in a Jackie Chan movie, where he put his back against one wall and 'walked' up the other, shifting every few paces like a lever. To do that, I had to put my phone back in my pocket, which was a task in itself. Pitch blackness again. Just me and Dead Erik, rotting quietly in the dark beside me.

The Jackie Chan worked for about four minutes. Or, if you want to look at it another way, for about five centimetres. Then I realized two things. Firstly, that I was nowhere near fit enough. Secondly, that Jackie had probably been wearing a pad under his outfit that meant his back didn't get ripped to shreds when he dragged it up his particular wall. My T-shirt was in no way up to the task. That stone was rough. Really rough. I tried to get through it. I gritted my teeth and braced my feet flat against that wall and I pushed.

I slipped. My legs folded as if someone had kicked me behind the knees and suddenly I was falling, brushing past the bones as I went. There wasn't far to go but there were only rocks and bits of Erik at the bottom. I slammed my tailbone on to one of the chunks of stone so hard that I was winded. I saw ghosts of stars at the edge of my vision, supernova bright but not really there.

It took me about ten minutes to get to my feet again. I hurt, every bit of me.

I dragged my phone out of my pocket. I'd just managed to thumb it on when a message blinked up: *20% power remaining.*

I think that was when I cried a bit.

# Chapter Thirty

Darkness is weird. Once you've been in it for a while, you think you can see things. Images started coming to me, a bit like the shock-star rainbows that I'd seen when I fell. Patterns that could only be in my head – chevrons, dots, wavy lines. One of them coalesced into a tree, just like the one I'd seen from my bedroom window the morning after the snow had started – white outlines against a black background.

I shivered. *Even here,* I thought. *Even here the firs can get me.*

I did try to pull myself together. Standing there, my legs growing more and more tired, my head growing heavier and heavier, I tried to work out where I was. I couldn't be far from the house. It must have been Dorothea who whacked me over the head so she couldn't have moved me far, even if the kid had helped.

I wondered why she hadn't left me in that secret

corridor. They could have locked it off and I'd never have been seen again. I thought it was probably because the walls were too thin. If I'd shouted, Dad and Mum might have heard me. And if I'd died, the smell...

Well, I knew what the smell would have been like. Although that kind of faded, with time. The thick stench of snails and rotting meat blended into the background. It became less important, the same as the darkness.

At first I stopped using my phone because I wanted to make the battery last. Then I realized that it didn't really matter. But anyway, I got used to the dark.

Kind of.

I shouted. I screamed. I cried and then I did all of those things again and again and again.

No one heard me. No one came.

After a while I lost track of how long I'd been there. I hadn't thought to look at the time when I'd first put my phone on and now it was dead. I'd used the last of the power to have one more look around my prison. Just in case.

The last thing I saw before the battery died was

Erik's bony, rotting face looking back at me.

So I stood there and I waited to die.

I don't know how long I'd been there before the light appeared. It flashed down the chute, blue white and blindingly bright, chased by an endless roar that split open the silence around me like an earthquake. I shut my eyes against the glare but I couldn't cover my ears to block out the noise. It went on and on, crashing down on me from above, crushing the last breath from my lungs.

I thought I was dead and whatever was happening was the next thing that happened to everyone. Maybe this exact same thing had happened to Erik.

Then something rested on my shoulder, a slight weight that pushed me away from the wall. I nearly faceplanted straight into Erik but instead the hard thing hooked itself under my armpit. It started pulling, a tug that dug into my shoulder blade as it dragged me up the wall.

The noise became colder. It hit me in the face with a thousand little pinpricks. The light moved away for a second, tipping sideways. I squinted upwards and saw two black shapes against the square white light of the open hatch. They were shapes I knew

– shoulders and heads and shouting mouths that I couldn't hear over the noise.

Mum and Dad.

The pinpricks of cold turned out to be snow. The blizzard was raging again, the rip and tear of it hollowing out my ears. I felt for a moment that I was being pulled out of a bottle and back into the real world, except that the real world was falling apart around us.

I must have blacked out for a second, because the next thing I remember is lying on my back in snow, with Mum and Dad leaning over me. My hands were free.

"Erik," I tried to shout, over the roaring of the storm. "It's Erik…"

They couldn't hear me. The wind ripped the words straight out of my mouth and threw them away into the storm. Dad was telling me something but I couldn't hear him. I realized he wasn't wearing a coat, which was really stupid in that weather. Then I realized it was because he'd wrapped it around me.

They started pulling me up. I couldn't stand on my own so they put an arm over each of their shoulders. Then I saw the boy. He was standing right in front of me, swamped in one of Mum's coats. I wanted to ask if they could see him, too, but in the end I didn't need to. He stumbled ahead of us into the house, which turned out to be right in front of us.

Inside, compared to the storm we'd been in, everything was quiet. I could hear the wind ripping around outside as if it were trying to get in but there was a buzzing in my ears, the kind of buzzing you only hear when there's nothing else going on. The door we came in through opened on to the pantry and that led into the kitchen. Everything was fuzzy and bright. They put me in one of the chairs beside the fireplace, the one next to the table with the tea set on it. As soon as I registered where I was – in Dorothea's chair – I got a bit fighty and tried to stand up again, so they found something else for me to sit on instead. Thinking about it now, I feel like this all happened in silence but it can't have done, can it? They must have been talking the whole time. I was probably talking, too, but all I can remember is the buzzing. And the light – light hurt, that was for sure. Dad put the overhead light on and it nearly blinded me, so he turned it off again and lit a candle instead. That made me think about the boy. I twisted round,

looking for him. I wanted to ask why he was there –
why we could all see him, where he'd been and how
he could still be alive but I don't remember asking
any of those questions out loud. I was probably
incoherent, I guess. Mum was crouching beside me,
trying to keep me still, stroking my legs and arms.
Dad was trying to look at my head. At one point he
tipped up my chin and looked into my eyes. Then, a
second later, he pulled me into a hug. I could still feel
Mum's arms across my legs, hugging the only bit of
me she could reach. I wanted to tell her I was glad she
was out of bed. I wanted to tell her she was looking
better, even though she wasn't really. But she was
there. She wasn't wherever she had been the last time
I'd tried to talk to her. She was there. *With me.*

Gradually sound started to come back. It
slowly began to overlay the buzzing. I could hear
murmuring. Their voices, talking to me. They got
louder and louder. I could hear someone gasping
for breath and realized after a few minutes that it
was me.

*You're all right,* they were both saying, over and
over. *You're all right now. We've got you. You're safe.
You're safe.*

It felt good to hear the words washing over me. My teeth were still chattering, so Dad added a blanket over his coat. Mum pushed something into my hands that turned out to be hot coffee. The drinking of it seemed to be less important than the holding of it. Eventually things started to get a little less hazy.

"It's all right," I heard Dad say again. "You're safe now."

"We've got you," Mum added.

I tried to say something but my jaw shook instead. I felt tired, so tired, but there were very important things trying to press their way out of my head. Erik. Dorothea. The boy.

He was still there, lurking behind Dad, staring at me with those huge eyes in his thin face. I blinked at him, wondering if he was going to disappear or turn into a wolf if I tried to keep him there in front of me but he didn't. Then I remembered that he was real. I remembered following him down the passageway, I remembered the nest of blankets inside the wall.

"Who are you?" Those ended up being the first words out of my mouth. "What's your n—" I stopped as my jaw shuddered and clamped shut again.

"Don't worry about that now," Dad said. "You need to get properly warm. I don't think, thank God, that you're concussed, or at least not severely. That's a nasty knock but you're in shock, more than anything."

I wasn't really listening. I was still watching the boy, who was watching me right back.

"But he's real," I said. "Who is he? What's he doing here? What—"

Mum leaned over me, her arms tightening around me. "Shh. We've all got a lot of questions. It can wait until you're feeling better."

I stared up at her and despite everything only one question really seemed important right then. "Are you all right now?" I asked.

I know it was a stupid question. I know these things don't magically fix themselves overnight. But she was here and she was talking to me. She had smiled at me and it didn't look fake. That had to mean something, right?

Mum smiled again. "Not quite," she said. "But I think that one day I might be."

We are the trees.
We are the snow.
We are the winter.

We will not forgive.

We will not.

# Chapter Thirty-One

The boy was Erik's son Ols. I don't know why I hadn't worked that out straight away. It seems so obvious now.

I was lying on the living-room sofa beside Mum when she told me. I'd fallen asleep and woken up to find myself there. Dad had carried me from the kitchen, she said.

"Dorothea killed his dad but kept him prisoner, poor little boy," Mum said. "She had him so scared that he still won't speak very much. I don't understand why. I don't understand any of it."

I did. It made perfect sense, in the most insane way. The Polaroids, Erik's last note. It all slotted together in my aching head to make a picture that was as complete as it was crazy.

Dorothea's plan to let the varulv get Erik for what he'd done to the forest hadn't worked. Worse than that, he'd worked out what was going on – or part of it. He'd sold up and had been preparing to leave the place for good so Dorothea killed him. But she still needed to make a sacrifice to appease the forest. *That*'s why she kept Ols.

Having us around must have complicated things, though. Poking our noses where we didn't belong. Finding out things we weren't supposed to know. Seeing things we shouldn't have seen.

I shivered. My skin was warm but something inside me wasn't. I'd dreamed of Erik's dead face. I realized that if we had left when the snow first started, with Tomas and the rest of the kids, Dorothea would probably have made Ols a sacrifice before now. But we had seen him.

"It was Ols upstairs in the attic. Wasn't it?" I said. "It must have been him you saw."

Mum nodded. "Yes. She was so angry with him for being spotted that she made him go out into the forest for a whole day. He was terrified that he was going to get eaten by wolves. And by then I was already doubting myself so I ended up believing that I'd ... I don't know, hallucinated him. And she kept saying things, whispering to me, making me feel worse..."

I got stuck on the 'sending him out into the forest' bit. That made sense. Because I'd seen him, hadn't I, that first day in the forest? So Dorothea had tried, at least. But for some reason the varulv hadn't taken him. Maybe they hadn't arrived by that point. The snow had started but only a little had fallen. Or maybe she had to find a way to let the varulv know there was a sacrifice ready...

That song, that weird haunting call. Had that been Dorothea? Was that what it was for, to call the varulv to the house?

"Where's Dad?" I asked. "And Dorothea? Where is she? She's really dangerous..."

Mum put her arm round my shoulder and squeezed me against her, kissing my head. She did it lightly but it still hurt. I didn't tell her that, though.

"It's all right," she said. "He's locked Dorothea in one of the bedrooms on the second floor. It seemed like the sensible thing to do, in the circumstances."

I tried to struggle upright again but my arms and legs felt heavy, as though they were made of lead. "You have to make sure there aren't any hidden doors," I said, breathless. "There are servants' passages all over this place, and—"

Mum gently pushed me back down. "Don't worry, Dad's checked. She can't get out, not on her own."

I lay back, exhausted again. "OK."

I shut my eyes, but Dead Erik's skull was still lurking behind my eyelids, so I opened them again. Then Dad appeared carrying a tray of steaming mugs. Ols followed behind him like a little shadow.

"Ah ha!" Dad said cheerily. "You're awake. Fancy a hot drink? I managed to find my way around that kitchen. What a warren…"

It felt surreal to sit there drinking hot chocolate as if everything was completely normal. I couldn't square it in my head with all the horrors that had happened since we'd arrived at Storaskogen. It's like when you have the first week of proper sun after a long winter and suddenly you can't remember the days ever being any different. It feels impossible that summer isn't going to last forever.

But it had happened. All of it had happened. Hadn't it?

"How did you find me?" I asked, pressing my fingers hard into the heat of the mug between my hands. "I screamed and I screamed. Did you hear me?"

"No," said Dad. "We have Ols and your mother to thank for that."

I racked my brain but couldn't remember anything after talking to Ols in the corridor. "Where was I? It was … it was a chute or something…"

"That's right," said Dad. "The old firewood chute down into the cellar. Dorothea didn't have to move you a long way. As far as we can work out, she dragged you on to the old tea trolley and pushed you through the pantry and out of the back door. The hatch isn't far from there."

"It's how she must have done it with…" Mum stopped herself and glanced self-consciously at Ols, "…the last time. But this time, Ols saw everything. He was such a brave boy. He came to get me, didn't you, sweetheart?"

Ols stared silently back at her over the rim of his mug.

Mum had been seeing him on and off ever since we'd got here. She'd thought she was losing it – going slowly nuts in this miserable, dark house at the end of the world. She'd assumed the little boy she'd spotted wandering the halls was a manifestation of her gathering insanity. She hadn't wanted to ignore him, though. So she'd started trying to talk to him. And the more she spoke to him, the more he appeared to her and the worse she felt.

I'm glad my mother is the kind of person who wants to make people feel included, even if they're ghosts. Mainly because if she'd just ignored him – if she'd shut her eyes and turned away in the hope that he would disappear and she could just forget – I'd probably be dead. I'd be still be jammed into that stone chute, rotting alongside Erik.

"Well," Mum said, "to be honest Ols didn't tell me anything. He just appeared by the bed, as silent as always. Except this time he reached out a hand and grabbed my sleeve. Can't tell you what a shock that was. All that time I'd thought he was made of light and shadows inside my head but he felt as real as you or me."

He'd kept tugging at her sleeve and pointing. Mum had woken Dad, who'd got a real shock when he saw a strange child standing there. Dad's reaction convinced Mum that Ols wasn't a hallucination. So they had followed the boy downstairs, listening to the blizzard ripping around outside. He'd led them to the kitchen, straight through it to the door and then right outside into the blizzard, to a hatch in the ground they could hardly see that was barely a metre from the back wall of the house.

He'd led them to me.

"What did the police say?" I asked. "You called them again, right? To tell them about … to tell them about what we've found? What happened to me?"

Dad glanced at Mum, who squeezed my shoulder. "We tried," he said. "The line's down. It must be the storm they said was coming – it's the worst we've had yet, I think."

He was probably right. I could hear it whining and moaning and hollering to get in. I shifted uneasily.

"But don't worry," he added. "We know they're on their way. They'll be here as soon as this weather front clears and we can tell them everything then. In fact, I've been thinking," Dad went on. "When you're feeling a bit better you should write down as much as you can. Everything you remember, whether it turns out to be relevant or not. That's always what the police say, isn't it? If you write it all down, you won't have to repeat everything over and over again."

That sounded like a pretty good idea to me.

# Chapter Thirty-Two

This is going to be the last thing I write about everything that's happened. It's been two days since they pulled me out of the chute and the storm is finally beginning to die down. The police should be here tomorrow. I've been writing every minute that I can. I've used that notebook of Erik's, the one I found the photographs in. It seemed a pity to waste it. My head is still aching from where Dorothea hit me and everything's been rushing to get out of it as quickly as it can. But at least they won't be able to say I've left anything out, will they? I've told them everything, even the bits that make me sound like a complete nutcase. So whatever happens from here on is their department. We'll soon be hundreds of miles away, back in Stockholm. Safe.

I'm sitting on my bed looking out of the window. The firs are still at the moment, covered with a thick blanket of snow that fell last night. They don't scare me so much now. I don't think it's nature we really have to be afraid of but other humans.

I think I went mad there, for a while, but I can see things more clearly now. I think writing it all down has helped me straighten everything out in my head. It can't possibly have been real, any of it. There were never any varulv. There definitely wasn't any girl who was also a wolf. There was only the snow and the trees and an old lady's crazy beliefs and a kind of mad waking dream that I fell into for a while because of all of the above. I guess at least I'll have something to tell Poppy and Lars when I get back to Stockholm.

I can hear Mum next door. She's reading Ols a bedtime story but I know that he won't sleep well. He has nightmares. He always dreams that the wolves are coming to take him away. Dorothea kept telling him that, over and over, and he can't stop himself believing it. Poor kid. I keep telling him that even if they were coming – even if they were real – it's fine. All we need to do is stay indoors, because the varulv can't get in anyway.

He says that's what his dad thought, too, but he'd been wrong. I can't really tell him that it wasn't the varulv that got his dad, it was Dorothea. It was all Dorothea. Even that boarded-up cellar. Dad went down to check it out, just to make sure there weren't any more nasty surprises lurking in the dark. It turns out that the reason she didn't want anyone going down there was because of Erik. The inner door she boarded up led to a corridor that would take you right into the kitchen cellar and to the chute where he was rotting. I guess the smell was so bad she didn't want to risk anyone going down there and getting a whiff.

Poor Erik. If only he'd left a few days sooner.

Dorothea's still locked up. Dad's tried talking to her — trust Dad — but she refuses. She does keep singing, though, which proves that it was definitely her making that weird noise. It twists through the house like ribbons of smoke but there's nothing we can do to stop her besides taping up her mouth. I suggested that but Mum and Dad won't do it.

There are wolves outside in the forest, too. Quite a lot of them, I think. I've heard them, howling as they prowl through the trees, although they stay too deep under the firs to be seen. I suppose Tomas was right about one thing after all. They're more afraid of us than we are of them.

I keep thinking about those people Erik thought were missing and wonder what really happened to them. Did any of them ever actually disappear? Or did they realize that they weren't cut out for living in this place and leave? I'll ask the police when they get here. But whatever they say, I'm not sure anyone will ever be able to get the truth out of Dorothea. She's like one of those trees out there, living in a world that doesn't meet up with ours any more. I wonder if it ever did. She's lived up here her whole life. The snow and isolation do funny things to your head, just the same way that darkness does. Here's what I think happened: she took one kid out into the forest, way back when the plantation was failing, when she was in love with her master and wanted to help him. Then things got better and she thought it had worked. So she ended up in a trap of her own making – she just had to keep doing it.

In some ways I'd like to think that those myths and legends are true. Not the way Dorothea believes in them, obviously. But the idea that there is a way to protect those things that the rest of us won't really ever understand; that wouldn't be a bad thing, would it? Someone's got to stand up for those things. Otherwise they'll be lost and forgotten and no one will care until it's far too late.

Maybe they're out there now, those forest spirits. Maybe they'll be out there long after the rest of us are all dead and gone, running through the snow until the end of the world.

Just as long as they stay out there, we'll all be fine.

The forest will not forget.

The forest will not forgive.

This is not an ending.
This is how it begins.

Payment is due.

# Appendix i

Friday 28 October 2016
2.44 p.m.

To: Bengtsonn.R@northernstarnewspapers.com
From: S.Norling@polisen.se

Mr Bengtsonn,

Please find attached the account and materials I mentioned when we spoke on the telephone last week. Forgive the length of time it has taken for me to send this on to you; locating it took longer than expected, as all materials associated with the case had been relocated to the 'cold cases' section following the closure of the original investigation. Cold investigations more than five years old are stored off site. I also hope you will forgive the somewhat haphazard nature of this PDF. Although a digital version of the original was transcribed at the time, this seems to have been misplaced. The attached PDF has been created from scans taken of the surviving notebook in which the account was written, which is still stored with the extant materials. It is mostly complete, but at some point the cover and initial page appears to have been lost.

As you can see, it is rather a long and sometimes strange account, written from a very personal perspective. However, it is by far the best introduction to what preceded the police visit to the property during the year that this document was written. Unfortunately it has provided very little clue as to what transpired once the author had finished writing.

Also included is a scanned version of the ledger mentioned in the document.

Despite thorough investigation at the time, the case remains unsolved.

I hope this will assist you in your research into the wider history of disappearances at Storaskogen.

Yours sincerely,

Ms Sira Norling
Deputy Chief Clerk
Pitea Police Department

# Appendix ii

Officer Marje Theorin, Pitea Police Department

Initial statement

28 November 2007

On the morning of 26 November 2007, I was one of four officers despatched to the house at Storaskogen plantation. The father of the family, Martin Stromberg, had contacted the police on the morning of 23 November 2007 to report that they required evacuation due to the early arrival of winter, a house fire and his wife's illness. We informed them that our arrival would be delayed due a storm that was forecast to enter their area.

Since I was on duty the day the call came in, Detective Chief Inspector Claesson asked me to do some background checking on both the Strombergs and the plantation prior to our departure. In carrying out this check, I found a report delivered by the hospital in Pitea detailing the arrival of a young girl called Alisa Svarssen who had been injured while part of a residential course at the forest in September 2007, shortly after the Strombergs' arrival at Storaskogen. There was also a police report indicating that at the beginning of October 2007 Martin Stromberg had filed a complaint in which he accused the injured girl's course leader of criminal damage.

On the morning of 26 November, DCI Claesson instructed me to contact Storaskogen by telephone to inform them of our departure and expected time of arrival. My attempts to contact the house by telephone were unsuccessful. During this period, the weather warning was upgraded to a severe blizzard in the area. DCI Claesson was not unduly concerned, judging that we would be able to leave again with the family before the storm reached Storaskogen.

Upon arrival at the property we noted that the front door of the house was standing open. Despite this and the noise of the helicopter landing, no one appeared to greet us.

On approach to the house, it became clear that the door had been standing open for some time, since the wind had blown a considerable amount of snow into the building. We entered, calling for the occupants to show themselves, but no one appeared.

The house was very cold. There were no fires burning in any of the grates we examined. DCI Claesson called for an initial search of the property but ordered me to stay with my partner, Officer Segersson. This search took approximately ninety minutes. We found no one inside the house.

There was no sign of violence or struggle apart from the remains of a conflagration in one of the bedrooms. As can be seen from the appended photograph, it seemed to have been extinguished by means of blankets, which were still piled over the initial incendiary point. This room also made clear that there were servants' passages in some parts of the house, since a large mirror was standing open, revealing the entrance to one such corridor. We searched these, too, but found no sign of the family or the housekeeper.

Having searched the house we attempted to search the surrounding area. The only tracks we found appeared to be canine (please see additional photographs appended), although it is possible that a fresh fall of snow had obscured any human prints.

The family's vehicle was still present.

We searched several outbuildings. There was no sign of human activity in any of these, although in one there was evidence of the damage that had prompted Martin Stromberg to file his initial complaint.

At the rear of the house, close to the back door that led into the kitchen, we located a chamber that appeared to be an old disused wood chute leading into a cellar. The cover had been recently lifted and then replaced, as it was still loose. Officer Segerson and I removed the cover. Inside the chute we discovered human remains in an advanced state of decay.

Following this discovery DCI Claesson recalled us to the house, which we searched again. During this search we discovered that the cellar into which the chute led had at one time been boarded up, as had the base of the chute itself (please see appended photographs). It was also during this new search that I located the document and what appeared to be a historical ledger. We found no further trace either of the Stromberg family or the housekeeper.

Eventually, aware of the time constraints imposed by the storm warning, DCI Claesson decided that we should return to Pitea pending a full investigation as soon as the weather would permit. He instructed us to photograph as much of the scene as possible prior to our departure.

We bagged several items that it was thought may pertain to such an investigation, including the document I had found and a series of photographs.

# Appendix iii

**Varulv (n.)**

A legendary spirit being specific to the folk traditions of northern Scandinavia.

*According to ancient folklore the varulv is a forest spirit, formed of the fusing between a human and a wolf, creating a creature that, although wolf-like in appearance, is neither true wolf nor true human. The creation occurs when a human is bitten by a varulv, causing the victim to become varulv in turn. The transition from human to varulv is said to result in a removal of human identity through memory loss, which according to certain traditions of the myth can only be restored when the varulv is called by its human name. If the varulv recalls its name, it can be returned to his or her former human self. If this restoration does not occur, the varulv will remain in its wolf-like state forever, as varulv are said to be immortal. Once the last living person to remember the varulv's former name is deceased, the varulv's fate is sealed forever.*

*Though most extant depictions of the varulv show them as fearsome creatures, they appear to have originally been* considered protectors of the great northern forests. The myth's origins are unclear, but it would seem they pre-date written language. The earliest written myths suggest that members of the community were given to the varulv as a spiritual offering to the trees; this offering would then allow the people dwelling amid those forests to do so successfully. One soul from each generation would be made varulv out of respect for the landscape; a sign of understanding that the human population dwelled there at the sufferance of older forces: the trees themselves. However, more sacrifices of the sort would need to be made in unusual circumstances, namely excessive destruction of the forest by human hands. Examples would include a population boom that required more wood be felled for extra homes or if devastation was caused by a human-set fire. To appease the forests, more members of the community – often, though not always, children – were sent to become ranks of the forest's protectors as both apology and appeasement. In this way it was believed that a balance was established between the forest and the people who lived within its borders. These sacrifices were made only once the first snows of winter had arrived.

It is supposed that the ancient legends of the varulv formed the antecedents of the modern populist fantasy of werewolves.

See also: **Kulning**

# Appendix iv

**Kulning (n.)**
An ancient Scandinavian vocal music form used as a herding call for its ability to travel great distances.

*Used most often in high mountain pastures where the sound is naturally amplified by the valleys and mountainsides on which the livestock would graze. Also used amid the great northern forests, both to gather livestock and to communicate with remote homesteads. Traditionally kulning calls would be distinct to families.*

*There is some suggestion that the call also deterred predators. Contradictory to this, however, other sources indicate that kulning was seen as a way to communicate with the spirits of the forest, for example when a community was ready to make a sacrifice. In this context the kulning was also used to restore a forest spirit to its full human state, as when answering the kulning call, the varulv enter a state of flux between human and wolf and can therefore understand the meaning of their human names should they hear them.*

*See also:* **Varulv**

# Acknowledgements

Firstly thanks must go to my wonderful agent Ella Kahn for believing enough in the bones of this book to encourage me to finish it and then finding the best home it could have at Stripes. Thank you to Ruth Bennett at Stripes for her editorial input and to Paul Coomey for designing such a striking cover. Many thanks to Margareta Olsson and Katarina Arnold for taking the time to read it for me and for their local knowledge. Lastly – although really he should be first, since without his support none of my books would exist – thank you to my husband Adam Newell, for the research road trips and constant encouragement.

Turn the page for an exclusive extract from

## BRYONY PEARCE

Coming for you in September 2017...

ISBN: 978-1-84715-827-7

# Where It All Started

"What would you do if you won a million pounds?"

There was something important behind Lizzie's question, I could tell by the way she kept twisting her short dark hair into knots as she showed us into her room. She was a ball of condensed energy, all excitement.

"You bring us up here for a quiz, Lizzie?" Grady asked as he dumped himself into a beanbag. He grinned at her as his knees almost hit his ears. Grady could be a bit … odd, but his smile was infectious; when he grinned, you grinned back.

I took a Coke from the six-pack I'd bought and passed the rest around. Carmen, who had already made herself at home and was lying on the bed, drank half of hers before Lizzie had the chance to open a can. My brother, Will, eyed his before taking it, as if wondering what I'd want from him later if he accepted.

I glanced at Lizzie as I put the spare can on her desk. "I thought we were heading into town?"

"This first. Take a seat." She switched on her computer, but didn't sit down, fidgeting on her feet.

As the monitor flickered into life I looked around. I hadn't been in Lizzie's room for years. When we were kids I was always here playing *Legend of Zelda* on her Wii. I hadn't realised how much I'd missed it.

"What happened to the 'no boys' rule?" Will slid into the chair by the desk and cocked his head, flicking his hair to the side. His pale brown hair looked almost grey in some lights, but Will prided himself on it. The way it was always hanging over his eye would drive me insane, but the girls liked it. Apparently.

"Seeing as I'll be at uni in a few months, Mum got reasonable." Lizzie smiled at me.

Her room hadn't changed a lot since I was last inside. The walls had been repainted, they were no longer baby pink but a light blue-grey; much more 'Lizzie'. The posters on the wall had morphed from Justin Bieber and Jonas Brothers into Nina Simone and Dean Martin – the old music she was always humming. But it was the same desk, I noticed as I ran my finger over our initials carved into the right-hand side, the same bed with the white ironwork, the same rug and even ... I looked harder ... yes, the same old red blanket that she used to wrap around her in the cold, folded neatly at the bottom of the bed.

I pushed Carmen's legs to one side and sat on the bed, one leg folded under me, just like I always used to.

"I'm so glad it's summer." Grady cracked open his can. "You guys are too, right? I mean, those exams!" He took a long drink. "Hey, you know Coke is the main cause of the US obesity epidemic? These cans contain, like, over forty milligrams of sodium. That makes you even thirstier, so you drink more. It's why there's so much sugar in it – to hide the salt."

I stared at him for a moment. "So, you don't want it?"

In answer Grady chugged the can. "It's about going into it with my eyes open. I can have a glass of water after." He burped and patted his belly.

Lizzie's eyes narrowed, but Carmen laughed. "You are too funny, Grady." I'd noticed that Will couldn't take his eyes off Carmen – she was wearing a tight T-shirt that said *Angel* across it.

"Do you guys want to see this or what?" Lizzie

turned her monitor so the rest of us could see the display.

Grady squinted at the old screen. "Why don't you get a decent system?" He frowned. "You know anyone could break through security on that dinosaur. They could be watching us right n—"

"Because we're so interesting?" I cut Grady off and ignored the way he folded his arms in response. I was trying to see what it was about the website on-screen that had Lizzie bouncing on her toes.

She pointed to a spinning logo.

Carmen glanced at her. "What's the Gold Foundation?"

"You know," Grady said, his irritation forgotten. "Marcus Gold – multi-billionaire. Owns half of Silicon Valley, runs all those charities, has that airline – Goldstar." He took a deep breath and carried on. "Rumoured to be part of Yale's *Skull and Bones* society. He's definitely a Freemason and probably one of the guys behind 9/11, he—"

Lizzie reached over Will and grabbed her mouse. "The only people behind 9/11 were the terrorists."

Will stayed quiet, but I noticed that he tilted his head to one side, watching curiously.

Grady sagged. "If you'd even look at the information I sent you—"

I rubbed my eyes. "Grady, David Icke thought he was the son of God. Why would you take anything he says seriously? We like you, but stop clogging up our inboxes with conspiracy-theory articles!"

Carmen peered at the screen. "What's Marcus Gold got to do with winning a million pounds?"

"Wait and you'll see." Lizzie moved the cursor. Under the Gold Foundation logo was another icon – *Iron Teen*, it read.

She clicked on it, leaned back and pressed her hands together. "Read that."

- Are you the best? Are you driven to succeed? Are you in top physical shape?
- Will you be between sixteen and twenty years old on 15th August 2017?
- Can you get a team together of five to six friends?
- Do you want to win £1 million pounds … each?

Under-eighteens need permission from a parent or guardian to apply.

Grady rolled off the beanbag and moved closer to the screen. "A million pounds *each*!"

I peered over his shoulder. "That's a six-million-pound prize!"

"That's what it says." Lizzie nodded excitedly.

Will frowned as if the text held a puzzle. "Why is Gold offering so much money?"

"He's a philanthropist," Lizzie said. Grady snorted loudly, but she ignored him. "Look, it says he wants to give bright, proactive teens a big push in life. Anyone can enter and it says the winners will receive investment advice to help them make the best of their prize money."

"Well, we don't have to *take* the advice," Grady said thoughtfully. "There's a lot I could do with that money."

Carmen began to skim read. "It says we have to fill in a load of assessment forms."

"But what's the *competition*?" Will put his hands behind his head and leaned back. "What do we have to do?"

Lizzie bounded forwards again. "We have to complete an assessment. The teams that qualify will go in a lottery to choose ten for the competition. The final ten teams will be flown out to a remote island that Gold owns, where there'll be tests of endurance and intelligence." She could barely supress her excitement. "It sounds like orienteering and puzzle-solving along with a bit of geo-caching, rock climbing … that kind of thing."

"That sounds great!" I said. I'd been failing to come up with anything to occupy me and Will over the shapeless summer ahead. "We'd enter even without the prize money, right Will?"

Will shrugged.

"There's nothing in here we can't do." Lizzie was almost dancing now. "If we pass the assessment and get through the lottery, then we could totally win this." She looked sideways at Carmen. "What do you think, Car?"

"I don't know, *tía*." Carmen frowned. "I'd have to take time off work."

"You enjoyed Duke of Edinburgh in the end." Lizzie's eyes sparkled with challenge.

"Huh. I liked helping at the animal shelter. But you promised we'd have a *fun* summer. This does not sound like fun."

"But a million pounds, Car." Will pushed his hair out of his eyes. "It would pay for vet school."

"That was private," she hissed, narrowing her

eyes at him. "A stupid dream."

"Only because you can't afford six years of uni," Will insisted.

"I can't afford *one* year of university, *estúpido*," Carmen snapped. "Why do you think I'm sweeping floors in a hairdresser?"

"We can't do it without you, Car." Lizzie sat on the bed next to me and put an arm around Carmen's shoulders. "We've got a team right here."

"Fine." She threw up her hands. "I can always get another floor-sweeping job if I lose this one."

"What about you, Grady?" Lizzie asked.

"I'm in if you guys are."

I felt a twinge of pity. Grady was lonely. We'd only let him join our Duke of Edinburgh squad because my mate Liam had dropped out at the last minute and Grady's dad, Doctor Jackson, had badgered my mum. He didn't yet trust that we were still hanging out with him because we wanted to. Plus Will seemed to like him, which was a definite bonus.

"So we're entering then?" I looked around.

Lizzie leaped to her feet. "This is going to be *amazing*, you guys." She clicked on the link to download the entry forms.

My phone blinked and started to vibrate. I checked the screen and bit my thumbnail. "Will – Mum's calling."

"She's calling *you*." Will didn't even look up.

I put down my drink, picked up the phone and went out to the landing. There was no telling what mood she'd be in. I took a deep breath, let the phone ring for as long as I dared and then accepted the call.

"Where are you?" she snapped.

"At Lizzie's."

"Will's with you?"

"Where else?"

"Don't take that tone with me." I could picture her sitting on the chair in the hall,. Her pale brown hair would be hanging half over her face – hers was more grey than Will's, but still, like his. Mine was ginger, like Dad's. "Are you watching him?"

"He's almost seventeen, Mum."

"He's … delicate."

Delicate my ass. I pulled the phone away from my mouth, sighed and returned it. "Yes, I'm watching him."

"You have to *be there* for him, Ben."

"Yes, Mum."

"He was the worst affected when your father left."

"OK, Mum."

Her tone changed. "You'd better not be eating anything over there. I've got your dinner on."

"Yes, Mum."

Will and I were only allowed to eat what she put on the table. This month we were 'doing Atkins'. I never thought I'd be nostalgic for carrots.

"*Yes, Mum. Yes, Mum.* Just like your father, you make promises then you go and do whatever you want." She was working herself up; probably standing now, pacing.

"Sorry."

I held the phone away from my ear as she began to yell at me. "… your responsibility, since your father left, don't you go thinking you're too good …"

I stopped listening and waited until her tone evened out again.

"Everything's fine here, Mum, honestly. No problems. We'll be back for dinner."

"Promise?"

"Why don't you make a cup of tea and have a lie-down. We'll let ourselves in."

"That's a good idea, Bennie." Her voice had

softened; she wanted to be looked after too.

Would she worry more when we left home in a few months, or less? She was the one who had allowed Will to do all his exams early and apply to Oxford at sixteen. She wanted to be able to boast about it. Selfish.

"I'll see you later, Mum."

Will looked up as I walked back in. "The usual?"

I tossed the phone on to the bed. "The usual."

The forms had to be filled in by hand and then posted, so Lizzie had printed them out. They'd all got started while I'd been on the phone. Carmen was humming tunelessly as she worked on hers. Clearly it wasn't just me who found it annoying, as Lizzie reached up from where she sat on her rug and switched on some music. Adele's honeyed voice filled the room and Will groaned.

"Do you think your mum'll let you come with us, Will?" Lizzie's fingers went back to her hair.

I wanted to catch her hand, to calm her. I gripped my pen tighter instead.

From his place at Lizzie's desk, where he was sharing the workspace with a kneeling Grady, Will looked up. "She'll be fine with it."

I snorted. "She won't be 'fine with it'. But Will should be able to talk her round. It would be easier if we could tell the papers we were applying – she'd love that. But the possibility of two million pounds should go a long way towards persuading her."

"I don't understand this dumb confidentiality clause – why can't we tell the papers?" Grady frowned. "It seems suspicious to me. If this was all above-board it would be everywhere."

"It's on the internet, Grady." Lizzie tapped her pencil impatiently. "It *is* everywhere."

"It's not a bad thing," I reminded him. "The fewer people know about the competition, the more chance *we* have of getting through the lottery."

"Do you really want to be in the papers saying 'we're entering this competition' then have to say 'but we lost' when the reporters follow up? Carmen looked up from her paperwork. "Or even worse, 'and we won'! If everyone found out, we'd be hounded for the money – it happened to my Uncle Javi."

"You have a millionaire uncle?" I gaped.

Carmen let out a laugh. "*Tío*! No! He won a year's supply of ham at the local festival. All he had, day and night, were calls from people wanting free ham."

She rolled off the bed. "I don't know my blood type, I need to call Mami. Can I use someone's phone?"

"Out of credit again?" Lizzie tossed hers over.

Carmen grinned. "Always." She danced into the hall and down the stairs. "*Buenos días*, Mrs Bellamy, you look lovely today," she called.

I started my own form while Carmen was out of the room, looking up when she flounced back and jumped on to the bed. "I'm O negative, by the way." She pulled her pages towards her and scribbled quickly.

"That's unusual, isn't it?" Lizzie adjusted her glasses.

"I am Spanish, remember?" Carmen said, as if that explained it.

"Actually," Grady said, "it means you're descended from the nephilm … or aliens. Opinion is divided on which it is. I'll send you a link."

Carmen grinned. "OK, *tío*, that sounds good."

Lizzie smiled behind her hand, then reached up and poked me. "Ben, have you got to Part Two? These questions are insane – listen to this. *Success is based on survival of the fittest; I don't care about the losers.*"

I frowned. "I'm not there yet…"

"What are we meant to answer though?" She pulled her glasses off. "I mean what do they want us to say? Look at these." She shoved her form at me.

**Choose the answer that most strongly reflects your opinion about each of the following statements. Please answer honestly.**

| | Strongly disagree | Slightly disagree | Neutral | Slightly agree | Strongly agree |
|---|---|---|---|---|---|
| Success is based on survival of the fittest; I don't care about the losers | | | | | |
| I find myself in the same kinds of trouble, time after time | | | | | |
| For me, what's right is whatever I can get away with | | | | | |
| In today's world, I feel justified in doing anything I can get away with to succeed | | | | | |
| I am often bored | | | | | |
| Before I do anything, I carefully consider the possible consequences | | | | | |

I pointed to the question at the bottom of the page. "That's easy – we have to agree, right? Show that we're going to think things through, not rush into dangerous situations."

"Carmen would have to lie then." Lizzie ducked as Carmen threw a pillow at her head. "Seriously though – I don't know what they want." She looked at Will. "What do you think? Should we tell the truth?"

Will folded his arms. "You're asking me if I think you should manipulate the system?" He grinned his Will-grin, a half-sardonic twist of the mouth.

I looked at my form. "You're really OK with cheating, Lizzie?"

"For a million pounds, are you kidding?" she cried.

I shook my head. "There are two *hundred* questions here. It's designed to trip us up if we're lying. And you don't know what they're really looking for in applicants – I think we need to answer honestly, like it says."

Will nodded. "Ben's right."

"*You* want to be honest?" Lizzie's eyes were round. "You – Will Harper? You only tell the truth when you can't be bothered to make up a decent fiction." She turned to Carmen, who flicked her pink-tipped hair over one shoulder. "Carmen?"

"It'll be easier to do it as myself, *tía*. More fun."

"I agree," Grady tossed his pen in the air but fumbled the catch.

"Of course you do," Lizzie muttered. "Fine. But I'm going to blame you guys if we get rejected before we even reach the lottery."

Turn the page for an exclusive extract from
the chilling prequel to *Frozen Charlotte*,

Coming for you in September 2017...

ISBN: 978-1-84715-840-6

The floorboards were like slabs of ice beneath my bare feet and my entire face ached with the effort of keeping my teeth from chattering as I made my way down the corridor. The candle in my hand shook, but I couldn't quite tell whether this was due to the dread I'd felt since the morning or the ghastly chill of the place. My nightdress and dressing gown felt like they were made from paper, for all the warmth they offered. The school was still and silent in the gloom and a coat of frost clung to the black windows, threatening to crack them.

I longed to return to my bed, climb beneath the covers and huddle there until the blood returned to my fingers and toes. But I had to know what was in that box. I simply had to. I'd recognized the spiked handwriting on the luggage label the moment I saw it – the unmistakeable slashed scrawl of a person I had hoped never to hear from again. A person who should be dead.

I made my way down the staircase, shielding the flame of the candle against the icy draughts that kept trying their very best to extinguish it. If it went out then I'd have no way of relighting it. I could feel the weight of the brass key to the luggage room in my pocket, where it had been sitting ever since I'd taken it from Mrs Carmichael's office. She'd be furious if she knew. She'd made it perfectly clear from the start that she didn't want a junior governess here, especially one who was only seventeen – not much older than the girls she lorded it over. I would surely be dismissed if she caught me.

I was just reaching for the door when I heard a muffled giggle. I stopped dead. The laugh had come from inside the luggage room. I stifled a groan. One of the girls must have got in there and decided to hide. Now I would have to deal with her and send her back to the dormitory before I could investigate the package. That's if Mrs Carmichael didn't wake up first and come storming downstairs, brandishing her crop at us for being out of bed.

I put the key in the lock and twisted it. The door creaked as it swung open and I peered into the darkness, the candle in my hand doing little to illuminate the room. The giggle came again, louder and sharper this time.

"All right, come out," I said in a clear, firm voice. "I know you're in here."

Nobody answered and I sighed. I was about to

speak again when I looked back at the door, key still stuck in the lock, and frowned. The door had been locked when I arrived, so how could a pupil have got inside in the first place? There was only one key, as far as I knew.

"Hello?" I called again.

In return there was nothing but thick, dusty silence.

Perhaps I had imagined that giggle after all? It might have been a mouse squeaking. One of the girls had said she could hear mice scrabbling in the walls just the other day, as I recalled.

I lifted the candle a little higher, straining to see through the shadows. The room was mostly filled with the girls' travel trunks, which were stored here during term time. The outline of a horse's head loomed out of the corner, giving me quite a start until I realized it was a rocking horse. There were some teddy bears next to it, along with a couple of dolls and a Jack-in-the-box. No doubt Mrs Carmichael had confiscated them from their owners as punishment for some trivial offence or other. There definitely wasn't a girl there.

I lost no time in locating the package, which was

still wrapped in brown paper, the school's address spelled out on the label in that hateful scrawl. There wasn't any doubt in my mind about whose writing it was. After all, I'd received enough scribbled notes in the past that the script was branded into my brain forever. I swallowed hard, set the candle down on the floor and reached out towards the brown paper with trembling hands. I'd intended to open it carefully so that I could attempt to wrap it up again, but now all I could think of was ripping it to shreds as quickly as possible to find out what was inside. My whole body shuddered with the possibilities.

I tore open the brown paper and it fell away to reveal a beautifully made toy chest, painted silver and black. My name, *Jemima*, was stamped across the front in carved wooden letters. I could feel a sob rising up in my chest at the sight of it. The nightmare was meant to be over. This school was supposed to be my fresh start.

My fingers fumbled with the clasp and I could hardly breathe as I lifted the lid. If there had been something as wretched as a severed limb or a rotting corpse inside I wouldn't have been surprised. So when I lifted the candle, I was startled to see that the box was filled with dozens of little china dolls.

They were all as pale as death – all except for one, which was completely black from head to toe, as dark and glossy as an oil slick. I reached out towards it, but as my fingertips brushed against another doll, I felt a sharp stab of pain and hurriedly snatched back my hand.

A bright bead of blood welled up on my finger and dripped on to a white doll, landing right where her heart would be, if she had one. I realized then that the dolls hadn't been well-packed for the journey and many of them had been damaged – an arm or a head or a leg snapped off, broken pieces rattling around at the bottom like bones. I'd managed to cut myself on one of the jagged edges of porcelain.

The dolls all had curly hair painted on their heads and painted shoes, and some of them even had stockings with blue ribbons. But it was their faces that disturbed me most. Their features were pretty enough, but their eyes were all closed. I suppose they could have been designed to look as if they were sleeping, but I knew, somehow, that it wasn't that. These dolls were supposed to be dead – I knew it as surely as if someone had just spoken the words in my ear…

Suddenly, I frowned. My eyes darted around the chest, looking for the black doll, but it was nowhere to be seen. It had been right on top before, standing out starkly among the white ones, and yet now it seemed to have vanished. There was a noise behind me and this time there was no mistaking it for anything other than what it was – a giggle.

I twisted round, still half crouched on the floor. "Who's there?" I cried.

The candle flickered, shadows shifting against the walls. There was someone in the room with me, I was quite certain of it. I turned back to the dolls and my breath caught in my throat. The black doll was right back where it had been before, perched on top of the others. I stared at it, my heart beating too fast and too hard in my chest.

Then I heard a voice, small and strange and shrill. *"Hide and go seek!"*

There was the sound of breath being blown out in one puff. The candle extinguished, filling the room with the scent of smoke and the cold horror of total, black darkness.

# FROZEN CHARLOTTE
ALEX BELL

ISBN: 978-1-84715-453-8

# SLEEPLESS
LOU MORGAN

ISBN: 978-1-84715-455-2

# DARK ROOM
TOM BECKER

ISBN: 978-1-84715-457-6

Some things are best left buried

# BAD BONES
GRAHAM MARKS

ISBN: 978-1-84715-454-5

# FLESH and BLOOD
SIMON CHESHIRE

ISBN: 978-1-84715-456-9

She's coming for you

# THE HAUNTING
ALEX BELL

ISBN: 978-1-84715-458-3

## Coming soon...

# CHARLOTTE SAYS
ALEX BELL

ISBN: 978-1-84715-840-6

Hunt or be hunted

# SAVAGE ISLAND
BRYONY PEARCE

ISBN: 978-1-84715-827-7

# RED EYE
Do you dare?